Hades

Also from Larissa Ione

~ DEMONICA/LORDS OF DELIVERANCE SERIES ~
Pleasure Unbound (Book 1)
Desire Unchained (Book 2)
Passion Unleashed (Book 3)
Ecstasy Unveiled (Book 4)
Eternity Embraced ebook (Book 4.5) (NOVELLA)
Sin Undone August (Book 5)
Eternal Rider (Book 6)
Supernatural Anthology (Book 6.5) (NOVELLA)
Immortal Rider (Book 7)
Lethal Rider (Book 8)
Rogue Rider (Book 9)
REAVER (Book 10)
AZAGOTH (Book 10.5)
REVENANT (Book 11)
HADES (Book 11.5)

~ MOONBOUND CLAN VAMPIRES SERIES ~
Bound By Night (book 1)
Chained By Night (book 2)

Hades

A Demonica Novella

By Larissa Ione

Hades
A Demonica Novella
By Larissa Ione

1001 Dark Nights

ISBN: 978-1-940887-55-5

Published by Evil Eye Concepts, Incorporated

Author Acknowledgments

Every story presents unique challenges for an author, and every story makes the author appreciate those who help to make a book the best it can be. For the most part, Hades played nice, but I need to thank Liz Berry, Kim Guidroz, and Pamela Jamison for all their hard work in whipping Hades into shape. I love you, ladies! I just wish Hades hadn't liked the whipping so much…

Sign up for the 1001 Dark Nights Newsletter
and be entered to win a Tiffany Key necklace.

There's a contest every month!

Go to www.1001DarkNights.com to subscribe.

As a bonus, all subscribers will receive a free
1001 Dark Nights story
The First Night
by Lexi Blake & M.J. Rose

One Thousand and One Dark Nights

Once upon a time, in the future…

I was a student fascinated with stories and learning. I studied philosophy, poetry, history, the occult, and the art and science of love and magic. I had a vast library at my father's home and collected thousands of volumes of fantastic tales.

I learned all about ancient races and bygone times. About myths and legends and dreams of all people through the millennium. And the more I read the stronger my imagination grew until I discovered that I was able to travel into the stories... to actually become part of them.

I wish I could say that I listened to my teacher and respected my gift, as I ought to have. If I had, I would not be telling you this tale now.
But I was foolhardy and confused, showing off with bravery.

One afternoon, curious about the myth of the Arabian Nights, I traveled back to ancient Persia to see for myself if it was true that every day Shahryar (Persian: شهريار*, "king") married a new virgin, and then sent yesterday's wife to be beheaded. It was written and I had read, that by the time he met Scheherazade, the vizier's daughter, he'd killed one thousand women.*

Something went wrong with my efforts. I arrived in the midst of the story and somehow exchanged places with Scheherazade – a phenomena that had never occurred before and that still to this day, I cannot explain.

Now I am trapped in that ancient past. I have taken on Scheherazade's life and the only way I can protect myself and stay alive is to do what she did to protect herself and stay alive.

Every night the King calls for me and listens as I spin tales. And when the evening ends and dawn breaks, I stop at a point that leaves him breathless and yearning for more. And so the King spares my life for one more day, so that he might hear the rest of my dark tale.

As soon as I finish a story... I begin a new one... like the one that you, dear reader, have before you now.

GLOSSARY

The Aegis—Society of human warriors dedicated to protecting the world from evil. Recent dissension among its ranks reduced its numbers and sent The Aegis in a new direction.

Emim—The wingless offspring of two fallen angels. *Emim* possess a variety of fallen angel powers, although the powers are generally weaker and more limited in scope.

Fallen Angel—Believed to be evil by most humans, fallen angels can be grouped into two categories: True Fallen and Unfallen. Unfallen angels have been cast from Heaven and are earthbound, living a life in which they are neither truly good nor truly evil. In this state, they can, rarely, earn their way back into Heaven. Or they can choose to enter Sheoul, the demon realm, in order to complete their fall and become True Fallens, taking their places as demons at Satan's side.

Harrowgate—Vertical portals, invisible to humans, which demons use to travel between locations on Earth and Sheoul. A very few beings can summon their own personal Harrowgates.

Inner Sanctum—A realm within Sheoul-gra that consists of 5 Rings, each containing the souls of demons categorized by their level of evil as defined by the Ufelskala. The Inner Sanctum is run by the fallen angel Hades and his staff of wardens, all fallen angels. Access to the Inner Sanctum is strictly limited, as the demons contained inside can take advantage of any outside object or living person in order to escape.

Memitim—Earthbound angels assigned to protect important humans called Primori. Memitim remain earthbound until they complete their duties, at which time they Ascend, earning their wings and entry into Heaven. See: Primori

Primori—Humans and demons whose lives are fated to affect the world in some crucial way.

Radiant—The most powerful class of Heavenly angel in existence.

Unlike other angels, a Radiant can wield unlimited power in all realms and can travel freely through Sheoul with very few exceptions. The designation is awarded only to one angel at a time. Two can never exist simultaneously, and they cannot be destroyed except by God or Satan.

Sheoul—Demon realm. Located on its own plane deep in the bowels of the Earth, accessible to most only by Harrowgates and hellmouths.

Sheoul-gra—A holding tank for demon souls. A realm that exists independently of Sheoul, it is overseen by Azagoth, also known as the Grim Reaper. Within Sheoul-gra is the Inner Sanctum, where demon souls go to be kept in torturous limbo until they can be reborn.

Sheoulic—Universal demon language spoken by all, although many species also speak their own language.

Shrowd—When angels travel through time, they exist within an impenetrable bubble known as a shrowd. While in the shrowd, angels are invisible and cannot interact with anyone — human, demon, or angel — outside the shrowd. Breaking out of the shrowd is a serious transgression that can, and has, resulted in execution.

Ter'taceo—Demons who can pass as human, either because their species is naturally human in appearance, or because they can shapeshift into human form.

Vyrm—The winged offspring of an angel and a fallen angel. More powerful than *emim*, *vyrm* also possess an ability that makes their very existence a threat to angels and fallen angels alike. With a mere second of eye contact, a *vyrm* can wipe out a fallen angel or an angel's entire immediate family. Once hunted ruthlessly, they are now a protected class, by mutual agreement between Sheoul and Heaven, so long as none harm others with their unique power.

Watchers—Individuals assigned to keep an eye on the Four Horsemen. As part of the agreement forged during the original negotiations between angels and demons that led to Ares, Reseph, Limos, and Thanatos being cursed to spearhead the Apocalypse, one Watcher is an angel, the other is a fallen angel. Neither Watcher may directly assist any Horseman's efforts to either start or stop

Armageddon, but they can lend a hand behind the scenes. Doing so, however, may have them walking a fine line that, to cross, could prove worse than fatal.

Ufelskala—A scoring system for demons, based on their degree of evil. All supernatural creatures and evil humans can be categorized into the five Tiers, with the Fifth Tier comprising of the worst of the wicked.

Chapter One

The road to Hades is easiest to travel. —Diogenes Laertius

Enjoy the trip, because the stay is going to be hell. —Hades

If Cataclysm had to clean one more toilet in this demon purgatory known as Sheoul-gra, she was going to jump in and flush herself down.

She'd always assumed that when angels got kicked out of Heaven they got to do fun fallen angel stuff. Like terrorize religious people and drink foamy mugs of Pestilence ale with demons. But no, she'd gotten stuck wiping the Grim Reaper's ass.

Okay, she didn't *actually* wipe Azagoth's ass. And if she did, his mate, Lilliana, would have had something to say about it. And by "say," Lilliana meant "behead."

Cat reconsidered that. Lilliana, who was still, technically, a fully-haloed angel, wouldn't do anything quite so drastic. Most likely. But Cat still wouldn't want to get on the female's shit list. Anyone who pissed off Lilliana pissed off the Grim Reaper, and that...well, Cat could think of nothing worse.

Except maybe cleaning toilets.

Stop whining. You took the job willingly.

Yes, that was true, but she'd only agreed to serve Azagoth because she wanted to earn her way back into Heaven, and doing that required her to A) keep her nose clean, B) avoid entering Sheoul, the demon realm humans often referred to as Hell, and C) do something heroic to save the world.

Easy peasy.

She snorted to herself as she carried a tray of dirty dishes from Azagoth and Lilliana's bedroom, her bare feet slapping on the cold stone floor that covered every inch of the ancient Greek-style mansion. He'd surprised Lilliana with breakfast in bed this morning, which was something Cat would have been shocked by a few months ago. Who would have thought that the Grim Reaper was such a softie?

She supposed she should have known better after he gave her a job and a place to live so she didn't have to worry about some jerk dragging her, against her will, into Sheoul for fun or profit.

No, Sheoul was off limits to her. Entering the demon realm would complete her fall from grace and turn her into a True Fallen, a fallen angel with no hope of redemption. As an Unfallen, she had a little wiggle room, but even so, very few angels had ever been given their wings back. In fact, she knew of only two

One of those two, Reaver, was now not only an angel, but one of the most powerful angels to have ever existed. His mate, Harvester, had also spent time as a fallen angel, but her circumstances were unique, and while Cat didn't know the whole story, she knew that Harvester had saved Heaven and Earth, and she deserved every one of her feathers she got back.

The thought of being made whole again made Cat's useless wing anchors in her back itch. Her luxurious mink-brown wings were gone, sliced off in a brutal ceremony, and with them, her source of power. She totally understood why an Unfallen would cross the barrier between the human and demon realms to turn themselves into True Fallen and gain new wings and new powers. But was the evil upgrade worth it? Cat didn't think so.

"Cat!" Azagoth's voice startled her out of her thoughts, and she nearly dropped the tray of dirty dishes as she looked up to see him striding down the hallway from his office.

In the flickering light cast by the iron wall sconces, he didn't look happy. He also wasn't alone.

Hades, Azagoth's second-in-command and the designated Jailor of the Dead, was walking next to him. No, not walking. With the way his thigh muscles flexed in those form-fitting black pants with every silent step, it was more like prowling. His body sang with barely-leashed power, and she shivered in primal, feminine response.

Son of a bitch, Hades was hot. Hard-cut cheekbones and a firm, square jaw gave him a rugged appearance that bordered on sinister, especially when paired with a blue Mohawk she'd kill to run her palm over. But then, she'd kill to run her palms over all of him, and she'd start with his muscular chest, which was usually, temptingly, bare. Not that she'd complain about what he was wearing now, a sleeveless, color-shifting top that clung to his rock-hard abs.

She tried not to stare, but really, even if she'd stood in the middle of the hall with her tongue hanging out, it wouldn't have mattered. He never looked her way. He never noticed her. She was nothing to him. Not even worth a glance. Those cold, ice-blue eyes looked right through her. And yet, this was a guy who laughed with Lilliana, pulled pranks on the other Unfallen who lived here, and played with hellhounds as if they were giant puppies. Giant, man-eating puppies.

Azagoth stopped in front of her. "Cat? You okay?"

She blinked, realized she'd been lost in a world of Hades. "Ah, yes. Sorry, sir. What is it?"

"Have you seen Zhubaal?"

She nodded. "He was heading toward the dorms about half an hour ago. I think he said he was going to be teaching some of the new Unfallen how to be an asshole or something."

Hades barked out a laugh, and she caught a glimpse of two pearly-white fangs. She used to think fangs were repulsive, but if Hades wanted to sink his canines into her, she'd gladly bare her throat and invite him in. She tapped her tongue against her own tiny fangs, the smaller versions that Unfallen grew a few days after being de-winged. For the most part, she'd gotten used to them. She didn't even bite her lip anymore.

"Z is finally teaching them something he knows all about," Hades said.

There was no love lost between those two, but Cat had no idea why. She did, however, know why *she* thought Zhubaal was an ass. Not that she wanted to think about it, let alone talk about it. She just had to hope that no one else knew.

Because humiliating.

"Thank you, Cataclysm," Azagoth said, dipping his dark head in acknowledgment. "I hear you've been helping out with the Unfallen, as well. Lilliana says you advised them to use their Heavenly names instead of their Fallen names. You know that's forbidden, right?"

Anxiety flared, but she lifted her chin and boldly met his gaze. "Not in Sheoul-gra. The rules are different in your realm. I figured that if they use their Heavenly names here, it'll remind them to stay on the right track if they want to earn their way back into Heaven."

Hades's gaze bored into her, the intelligence in his eyes sparking. No doubt he was wondering why she hadn't taken her own advice, but thankfully he didn't have a chance to ask.

"Very smart." Azagoth's approval gave her a secret thrill, and then it was back to minion-chores as usual when he said, "By the way, my office could use some attention. It's a little...messy."

Azagoth brushed past her, and was it her imagination or did Hades linger for just a moment? Every inch of skin exposed by her blue and black corset tingled, and she could have sworn his gaze swept over her, appreciative and hot. But then he was as cold as ever, walking next to Azagoth as if she didn't exist and never had.

With a sigh, she dropped off the dishes in the kitchen and grabbed her bucket of cleaning supplies before heading to Azagoth's office. Once inside...well, he wasn't kidding when he said he'd left a mess.

She ran a cloth over the stone and wood walls, wiping down the blood mist from whatever demon Azagoth had vaporized. And it must have been a *big* demon.

Apparently, he didn't obliterate demons often; there was a price to pay for destroying souls. But when he did, the mess was considerable.

She went through two bottles of cleaner and dozens of rags before the office no longer resembled a slaughterhouse, and man, she was going to need a long shower. Relieved to finally be done, she started to gather her supplies when a dark spot on the wall behind Azagoth's desk caught her eye. Cursing, she swept her cloth over the stain, scrubbing to make sure she got every sticky bit of gore. But dammit, blood had gotten into a crack, and...she frowned.

Putting down the rag, she traced the crack with her finger, squinting at what appeared to be a round recess in the wall. What the heck was it? Driven by curiosity, she pushed slightly. There was a click, followed by a flood of light coming from behind her.

Oh...*shit.*

She turned slowly, and her gut plummeted to her feet.

A huge chunk of wall had disappeared, revealing a portal from the human and demon planes. A stream of *griminions* filed through, their short, stocky forms escorting the souls of demons and evil humans into the realm of Sheoul-gra. The creepy little *griminions* chittered from under their black, monk-like hooded robes as they marched the souls, whose bodies in Sheoul-gra were as corporeal as her own, through the cross-sectioned tunnel, only to disappear into another portal that would take the demons to their final destination—Hades's Inner Sanctum.

"No!" she shouted. "Stop! Azagoth hasn't approved the

transfers!"

But they didn't stop. They kept emerging from the right side of the tunnel and disappearing through the shimmering barrier of darkness to the left. Panicked, she pushed on the lever again, but the *griminions* kept marching. She wiggled it, pushed harder, punched it, and finally, with a whoosh, the portal closed, leaving only a solid wall in its place.

Cat swallowed dryly, her heart pounding, her pulse throbbing in her ears. Maybe she hadn't screwed up badly enough for anyone to know. Maybe no one would notice the souls that got through to the Inner Sanctum without Azagoth's approval.

And maybe she'd just earned herself a place in the Grim Reaper's hall of horrors, the Hall of Souls at the mansion's entrance, where statues made out of the bodies of his enemies were on display for the world to see.

What made it all worse was that the people encased in those statues weren't dead.

On the verge of hyperventilating, she slumped against Azagoth's behemoth of a desk and forced herself to breathe slowly. How did she keep screwing up? And not just screwing up, but *royally* screwing up. Just last week she'd broken one of Azagoth's centuries-old Japanese swords. And a month before that, she'd spilled pineapple soda all over a priceless rug woven from demon sheep wool by Oni craftsmen.

"Did you know that, unlike pineapple soda, fallen angel blood doesn't stain demon wool?" he'd asked in a dark, ominous voice as she'd scrubbed the rug. And no, as a matter of fact, she hadn't known that.

When she'd said as much, he'd merely smiled, which was far, far worse than if he'd just come out and said that if she fucked up again, her blood would definitely *not* stain that damned carpet.

Soda, however, did stain, just like he'd said.

It seemed to take hours before she stopped trembling enough to gather her crap and flee the office, and thankfully she didn't run into Azagoth on her way to her quarters. She did manage to catch another glimpse of Hades as he rounded a corner though, the hard globes of his ass flexing under the tight, midnight black pants.

Maybe she could try talking to him someday. Try saying something more coherent than, "Hi, Mr., um, Hades. Or do you prefer Jailor? Or Lord? Or...?"

He'd looked at her as if she'd crawled out of a viper pit. "Hades," he rumbled. "Easy enough."

And that had been the sum of their conversation. Their only conversation. Ever.

Did he think she had freaking halo pox or demonic measles? And why was she dwelling on this anyway? He was clearly not interested in her, and she had more important things to worry about.

Like whether or not Azagoth was going to *not* stain his carpet with her blood when he found out that she'd allowed unauthorized souls to enter the Inner Sanctum.

Chapter Two

Hades had a lot of names. Lord of the Dead. Keeper of Souls. Jailor of the Baddies. Asshole.

He owned them all. Ruled his piece of the underworld with an iron fist. Feared nothing.

Correction. He feared nothing except the Grim Reaper. Azagoth was the one person who had proven time and time again that he could turn Hades's underworld upside down and shake it like a snow globe.

So Hades generally despised the monthly meetings between him and Azagoth, but thankfully, this latest one had been refreshingly brief and light on fault-finding. Which was good, because Hades's brain had been occupied with images of Cat.

He remembered the first time he'd seen her when she came to work for Azagoth a few months ago, remembered how drawn he'd been to her energy. She was new to life on this side of the Pearly Gates, and while most newly fallen angels were either terrified or bitter, she was neither. According to Lilliana, Cat was curious. Eager to learn. Enthusiastic to experience new things.

Hades could teach her a new thing or two.

Except he couldn't, could he? Nope, because the curvy redhead was off-limits to him, and panting after her like a hellhound on the trail of a hellbitch in heat would only end in pain.

Pain that would likely come at the end of Azagoth's hand, and Hades had long ago learned that pissing off his boss was stupid beyond stupid...beyond stupid.

Still, it grated on him that he'd been read the riot act about Cat when he was about ninety-nine percent sure Zhubaal had bedded her. So what was up with *that*? Z was a cranky sonofabitch with a short fuse and a stick up his ass, but somehow *that* mongrel was good enough for Cat?

So fucked up.

Hades took one of three portals dedicated to travel between Azagoth's realm and the Inner Sanctum back to his residence, and as he materialized inside his living space a tingle of mayhem skittered over his skin. How...odd. Sure, hell was all about mayhem, but this was different, and it had been different for a few months now. Before, there had always been a balanced mix of order and chaos. Organized chaos. Chaotic organization.

Even here, in Sheoul-gra's Inner Sanctum, where the souls of dead demons came to play until they were born again, there was order. Rarely, there was chaos.

At least, chaos used to be rare. But now that Satan had been imprisoned and Sheoul was no longer under his rule, all hell had broken loose—literally. Sheoul was now operating under a new regime, with a dark angel named Revenant as its overlord, and not everyone was happy about the new leadership situation. Just as with humans, demons didn't accept change easily, and the tension surrounding Revenant's takeover had bled over into Sheoul-gra.

Completely unacceptable.

The tingle began to sting, as if Hades was crawling with hornets. Resisting the urge to rip off his own skin, he stepped into his personal portal next to the fireplace. Like Harrowgates that transported demons around Sheoul and the human realm, some of the portals inside the Inner Sanctum had been built to travel only between two locations, while others could transport a person to one of multiple places by manipulation of the symbols inside the portal's four walls. But Hades could also operate them with his mind, allowing any portal to take him anyplace within the Inner Sanctum he wished to be. Or, like now, to get where he needed to be, he merely had to concentrate on the sensation of mayhem wracking his body, and a moment later, the portal opened up.

He wasn't at all surprised to find himself in a burned-out sector of the 5th Ring, a vast, dreary realm of fog, heat, and despair that contained the evilest of the evil. Before him, demons scattered into the mist the moment they recognized him.

Most demons, anyway. A few stood their ground, their defiance admirable, if not foolish.

A demon who had been a professional torturer before he was

killed several years ago by Aegis demon slayers blocked his path. Here, demons could choose their appearance, and this bastard had chosen his former skeletal Soulshredder form, his grotesque, serrated claws extending from long fingers.

"Move." Hades slowed, but he didn't stop. He didn't have time for this shit. His skin burned and his insides vibrated, alerting him to some sort of violent disturbance nearby. And it had to be a whopper for him to have felt it from inside his home on the other side of the Inner Sanctum...which was roughly the distance from one earthly pole to the other.

"Fuck you, Soul Keeper."

Surprise jolted him; few were brave—or stupid—enough to challenge him. But Hades kept his expression carefully schooled. Tension was running high right now, and he couldn't afford to let anyone think he was losing control of the Gra.

From two-dozen feet away and without breaking his stride, Hades flayed the demon with a mere thought. Stripped him of his skin like a banana. The demon screamed in agony, and Hades let him. That noise would carry for miles, warning everyone within earshot of the consequences of fucking with him. Sure, Hades could have "killed" him, but the demon's soul would simply have fled the old, broken body and taken a new form. Handing down pain was much more satisfying.

Hades continued on his way, his boots crunching down on charred bone and wood, and as he strode by the Soulshredder, the demon stopped his annoying screaming long enough to croak, "You...will...fail."

Hades ignored him. Because really? Fail at what? His job was pretty simple and straightforward. All he had to do was keep demon and evil human souls inside the Inner Sanctum until the time came when, or if, they were born again. *How* he kept them was entirely up to him. He could leave them in peace, he could torture them, he could do whatever he wanted. Failure? That was ridiculous. There was nothing to fail *at*.

Really, this place was boring as shit most of the time.

Leaving the asshole behind, he threaded his way past the kind of horrors one would expect to find in a place where the evilest of evils lived, but the bodies, blood, and wrecked buildings didn't even draw his eye. He'd seen it all in his thousands of years down here, and nothing could faze him.

Not even the hellhound crouched in the shadows of the gnarled thorn tree gave him pause. The beasts could cross the barrier between Sheoul-gra and Sheoul, and for the most part, Hades let them. He kind of had to, since their king, Cerberus, had taken it upon himself to be the self-appointed guardian of the underworld—specifically, Sheoul-gra. For some reason, hellhounds hated the dead and were one of the few species that could see them outside of Sheoul-gra. Inside Sheoul-gra, they got their rocks off by ripping people apart. As long as they limited their activities to the 3rd, 4th, and 5th Rings, where the worst of the demons lived, he didn't give a crap what the fleabag hounds did.

Ahead, from inside the ruins of an ancient temple, came a chorus of chanting voices. *Ich tun esay. Ich tun esay. Ich tun esay alet!*

He frowned, recognizing the language as Sheoulic, but the dialect was unfamiliar, leaving some of the words open to interpretation. Somehow, Hades doubted his interpretation was correct and that the chanters were talking about opening a dime store.

He tracked the sound, and as he approached the reddish glow seeping through a doorway in the building ahead, the hair on the back of his neck stood up. What the hell? He hadn't been creeped out or afraid of anything in centuries. Many centuries.

Ich tun esay. Ich tun esay. Ich tun esay alet...blodflesh!

What. The. Fuck.

Something screamed, a soul-deep, tortured sound that made Hades's flesh crawl. Something was very, very wrong.

Kicking himself into high gear, Hades sprinted into the fire-lit, cavernous room...and then he skidded to a halt, his boots slipping in pools of blood on the stone floor. A hundred demons from dozens of species were gathered around a giant iron pot hanging over a fire. Inside the pot, a Neethul demon's screams died as his body bubbled in some sort of acidic liquid.

"*Stop!*" Hades didn't give a shit about the demon. What he did give a shit about was the ritual. In Sheoul-gra, all rituals were forbidden and came with a penalty of having one's soul disintegrated, so they didn't happen often. Oh, Hades had come across one or two loners performing religious rituals now and then, but this kind of massive gathering and ceremony? This was a first.

And, by Azagoth's balls, it would be the last.

The mass of chanting demons turned as a unit, their creepy smiles and empty eyes filling him with a sickening sense of doom. Alarm shot through him, and in an instant, he summoned his power and prepared to blast every one of these freaks into the Rot, the prison meant for the worst of the worst, where suffering was more than legend, and where the only release came when Azagoth destroyed your soul.

With a word, he released his power. At the same moment, one of the demons overturned the pot of acid. The liquid, mixed with the goo of the dissolved Neethul, splashed on the floor in a whoosh of steam. Suddenly, as if Hades's power had hit an invisible wall, it bounced back at him, wrapping him in a cocoon of blackness.

As he was transported by his own spell to the prison all demons feared, he heard the chant again. *Ich tun esay alet!*

Oh...shit. This time, he understood.

The demons weren't trying to open a dime store. Somehow they'd acquired a forbidden object or person of power and were attempting to open Sheoul-gra's very walls, to allow millions of souls out into the human and demon realms.

They were looking to feast.

Chapter Three

Hades had no trouble freeing himself from the Rot, although he'd had a hell of a time trying to convince one of the guards, a fallen angel named Vype, that he wasn't a demon in disguise.

Once he'd talked the guy down, Hades gathered a handful of his fallen angel staff and returned to the site of the demonic ritual. Within a few hours, they'd captured two of the demons who had been there. They'd changed their physical appearances, but Hades could see through their costumes to their souls. Idiots.

After delivering them to the Rot, he went immediately to Azagoth, who was surveying his library's vast shelves of books, some of which vibrated as his gaze landed on them. Hades hung back, a lesson learned after being bitten by one of Azagoth's rabid tomes. Who knew books could bite? Vicious little bastards.

Hades cleared his throat to announce his presence. Azagoth didn't even turn around, simply barked out a curt, "Sit."

The Grim Reaper's voice didn't leave room for argument. But then, it rarely did. So Hades took a seat in the leather chair...leather made from the finest Molegra demon hides.

Azagoth took a seat on the plush sofa across from Hades and reached for a tattered book on the armrest. "So," he said. "What's going on in the 5th Ring?"

Hades didn't bother asking how Azagoth knew. No doubt one or more of Hades's wardens were agents for Azagoth. The guy's spy network extended from the deepest pits of Sheoul to the highest reaches of Heaven.

"Hell if I know," Hades said. "But whatever it is, it's bad. I caught a bunch of assholes performing a forbidden ritual powerful enough to deflect my power and blast me to my own fucking prison."

One of Azagoth's dark eyebrows shot up. "I assume you took care of the situation."

"Once I got myself out of my own jail, yeah. I only found two of the offenders, but I've got 'em strung up and awaiting your questioning. I believe they got their hands on something from outside. The power they wielded was like nothing else I've felt."

"Dammit," Azagoth breathed. "You're losing control—"

"My ass," Hades snapped. "The Gra is becoming overloaded with evil souls. You need to stop reincarnating only non-evil demons and start working on the baddies. Get them back to Sheoul where they belong. I've been spending way too much time moving Ufelskala Tier 4 and 5 demons to Rings less equipped to handle that kind of malevolence."

The Ufelskala, a scale developed to categorize demons into five Tiers based on the intensity of evil inherent to their species, was also one of the tools Azagoth used to sort demons into the five Rings of the Inner Sanctum. Not that the guy couldn't send anyone to any Ring he wanted, but in general, he followed the information laid out in the Ufelskala.

"The 1st and 2nd Rings are clearing out," Azagoth said. "As per Revenant's orders, I'm reincarnating a lot of the non-evil demons on those levels. So do some creative reassigning."

Not only would that be a lot of work, but it would require bringing in more fallen angels to oversee Rings that were going to contain a lot more evil demons, and no fallen angel volunteered to work in the Inner Sanctum. Not when they weren't allowed to leave and their powers were limited. They'd have to be...recruited. By force.

"Sir, this is bullshit," Hades growled. "What the everloving fuck is Hell's new overlord doing?"

Azagoth flipped open the book. "That's not for you to question."

Hades burst to his feet. "My hot ass," he snapped. "I never thought I'd say this, but at least Satan kept order and balance in Sheoul. This new douchebag—"

Burning pain ripped through him, and only belatedly did he realize that he'd been struck by a bolt of hellfire that had streamed directly from Azagoth's fingers.

"Here's the thing," Azagoth said calmly. "Satan didn't give a shit what anyone said about him. But Revenant? He's putting down everyone who speaks out against him. Hell, he's laying out anyone he even *suspects* might rebel."

"That's because he's a paranoid fool. Learning his true identity has made him weak." Apparently, Revenant had grown up in Sheoul believing he was a fallen angel, when the truth was that he had always been a Heavenly angel. How could a true angel, no matter how tarnished his halo, expect to be ruthless enough to rule Hell?

"And yet, he managed to defeat and imprison not only Satan, but Lucifer, Gethel, and the archangel Raphael as well." Azagoth snapped the book closed with a heavy thud. "Respect him."

"He couldn't have done it without help from his brother," Hades muttered.

"Maybe not. But keep in mind that he and his brother have each other's backs. Don't piss off either one of them. Together they are far more dangerous than Satan ever was."

Hades actually liked Revenant's brother, Reaver, who happened to be one of the most powerful Heavenly angels to ever exist. Reaver had spent a little time in the Inner Sanctum as Azagoth and Hades's prisoner, and really, even when the guy had been in pain, he'd been pretty cool.

But Revenant could suck Hades's balls.

The thought of having his balls sucked made an image of Cat flash in his head, which, granted, was way better than thinking of Revenant. But still, off-limits was off-limits. Dammit.

"Yeah, whatever," Hades said, resisting the urge to roll his eyes. "Ever since Rev took over as King of Hell, the Inner Sanctum has been a war zone."

"Which is, in part, because he requested that I only reincarnate Ufelskala Tier one and two demons."

"And the result of that idiotic order is that my domain is filling up with majorly evil fuckheads who only want to cause trouble."

Azagoth's dark eyes flashed as his patience with Hades wore thin. But then, he'd never had much patience to begin with. "Deal with it. Now. Your rebellions are leaking over into my part of Sheoul-gra, and the archangels are starting to get twitchy."

"The *archangels* are starting to get twitchy? I'm the one trapped down there with demons who are desperate to get out."

"Then keep it from happening."

Keep it from happening? As if Hades had just been laying around on a beach and drinking margaritas while the Inner Sanctum went up in flames? "What the fuck do you think I've been doing for thousands of years?"

There was a long, brittle silence, and then Azagoth's voice went low. And maybe a little judgmental. "There have been escapes."

"Very few, and never more than one at a time. And come on...there were special circumstances in each case." No demon could escape on his own, not when demons had no power in Sheoul-gra. Escape required energy or objects from an outside source, which was why visitors were very rarely allowed inside the Inner Sanctum. A single feather from an angel could be used in spells to destroy barriers or kill a target. One seemingly harmless vampire fang had once given a Neethul the power to reincarnate himself without Azagoth's help.

"Still, you must be extra vigilant." Azagoth dragged his hand through his black hair, looking suddenly tired. Good. Hades shouldn't be carrying the stress of all of this by himself. "I've never seen Sheoul so unstable."

Vigilant. *Vigilant*, he'd said. As if Hades was a total noob at this. But instead of saying that, he merely gritted his teeth and offered a tense smile. "Yes, sir. Anything you say, sir."

"Good. Now get out. And do not fail me again."

* * * *

Somewhere outside Azagoth's Greek-style mansion, a bird of prey screeched. Cat loved hearing it. Not long ago, Sheoul-gra had been a dead realm, a physical manifestation of Azagoth's emotional state. Dark and dreary, the "Gra," as it was sometimes called, had resembled a toxic wasteland that couldn't support any animal or plant life that wasn't straight out of Hell itself.

But Lilliana's love had changed Azagoth, and with it, his realm.

Now, when Cat strolled outside the palace, the grounds and buildings surrounding it teemed with life, from the lush grass, leafy green trees, and sparkling water, to rabbits, birds, and even the occasional fox or deer.

Smiling, she put down her feathered duster and headed from Azagoth's pool room toward the mansion's entrance, and as she rounded a corner, she collided with a body.

A huge, muscular body.

Hades.

An instant, hot tingle pricked her skin as she leaped backward, crashing into something behind her. She heard something break, but at the moment, it didn't matter.

This was the first time she'd touched Hades. The first time her ability to sense good and evil as a physical symptom on the surface of her skin had triggered. At least, it was the first time with Hades.

She'd always suspected he'd give off an intense blast of evil, but she hadn't expected the evil to be tempered by a ribbon of goodness. She also hadn't expected to be so...aroused by the vibes he gave off. Then again, merely looking at him aroused her, so why wouldn't touching him do the same?

He stood there, bare-chested and wearing a skin-tight pair of silver pants that showed every ropey muscle and presented that impressive bulge at his groin like a gift. Criminy, he might as well be naked. She *wished* he was naked.

"E-excuse me," she squeaked.

He looked down at her, one corner of his perfect mouth tipped up in a half-smile. Which was a first. Everyone seemed to get smiles but her.

"You broke Seth."

She blinked. "What?"

He nodded at something behind her. She turned and gasped in horror at the black, waxy hand lying on the floor and the now-handless statue next to it. "Oh, shit. Azagoth is going to be pissed."

This was his Hall of Souls, a giant room filled with mounted skulls and fountains that ran with blood. It was also where people who did especially vile things—or who made Azagoth *really* angry—were turned into tortured statues. Inside, they were still alive, screaming for all eternity. And she'd just given one an amputation that must be agonizing.

She scrambled to replace the hand, but Hades just laughed. "Don't worry about it. Seth was a demon who passed himself off as an Egyptian god back in the day. He tortured and killed thousands of children. He deserves worse than anything Azagoth or you could do to him."

She stared at the statue, the naked body twisted in whatever agony Azagoth put him through before turning him to stone, his mouth open in a perpetual scream.

"Children?"

"Children."

Sick bastard. She dropped the hand, grabbed Seth's tiny penis, and snapped it off. "I hope he's feeling that."

Hades's booming laughter echoed around the chamber, and she swore the crimson liquid in the center fountain stopped flowing for a heartbeat. "I'll bet you just made every poor stiff in here fear you more than Azagoth. Awesome."

She dropped the nasty appendage next to the hand. "Yeah, well, I'd probably better find some Superglue before he notices."

Hades nudged the pieces with his boot. "I'll take care of it. I'm the one who ran into you, and besides, I live for this kind of thing."

The note of mischief that crept into his voice made her suspicious, and she narrowed her eyes at him. "What have you got up your sleeve? You know, if you had sleeves."

"Don't worry," he said with impish delight, "I know what to do with a cock." He shifted his gaze to her, giving her a roguish once-over that heated her skin even more than touching him had. "So, what's got you in so much of a hurry? Hot date?"

Flustered, because this was the first time he'd spoken to her like she wasn't diseased, she stood there like an idiot before finally blurting, "I heard a bird."

He looked at her like she was daft. "And that's significant...why?"

Heat flooded her face. She must be as red as a Sora demon's butt. "They have wings." Geez, could she sound any dumber? "I guess I miss mine."

"If you miss them that much, you could just enter Sheoul." Massive black, leathery wings sprouted from his back and stretched high enough to brush the ceiling. Blue veins that matched his hair extended from the tips to where they disappeared behind his shoulders, and now that his wings were visible, the veining appeared under his skin, as well. It was as if he were a marble statue come to life.

Cat's breath caught in her throat as she took in his magnificence. He'd transformed, and for the first time, she could see why the demons in the Inner Sanctum would kneel before him.

I'd kneel, she thought, *but for far different reasons.*

That image burned itself into her brain, and she wondered if her face went even redder. Then, to her horror, she found herself reaching out to skim her fingertips along the edges of his wings. He went taut, but her body did the exact opposite as shivery, wild sensations jolted her system and coiled between her thighs. Damn, this male was a danger to everything that made her female, and she stumbled back on unsteady legs.

"Sorry," she whispered, hoping her voice didn't betray her lust.

"Like I said, I miss them. I want them back, but I want to get them by earning my way back to Heaven, and I can't do that if I become a True Fallen."

"Not joining me on the dark side, huh?" Now that she was no longer touching him, he'd relaxed, probably relieved that the crazy, horny Unfallen was keeping her hands to herself. Shrugging, he put away his wings, and the veins under his skin faded away. Good, because her fingers might have been all about his wings, but her tongue had wanted to trace every vibrant vein on his body. "Suit yourself. More evil cookies for me."

Shooting her a wink, he sauntered off toward one of the portals that allowed travel between Sheoul-gra proper and the Inner Sanctum. Cat watched him—and his drool-worthy butt—until he disappeared around a corner.

Outside, the bird of prey screeched again, but now that she'd seen Hades's wings, she wasn't sure anything else could compare. As she contemplated her next move, she eyed the castrated statue and, unbidden, her mind popped an image of the bulge in Hades's pants. She glanced down at the sad little male appendage on the floor and laughed.

Nope. No comparison.

Chapter Four

It had been three days since Cat had opened the portal from the human realm and allowed souls into the Inner Sanctum, and as far as she knew, nothing catastrophic had happened. Maybe no one had noticed. After all, there were millions of souls imprisoned in Sheoul-gra. So what if a handful had slipped through without Azagoth's stamp of approval?

Rationalizing the whole thing didn't make her feel a lot better, so she took out her frustration on the floor of the Great-Hall-slash-Hall-of-Souls at the entrance to Azagoth's mansion. Why the hell did she have to polish the obsidian stone by hand, anyway? Did Azagoth not believe in buffing machines?

Okay, in all fairness, he'd never told her to clean the floor. The big jobs, like landscaping outside and maintaining the floors inside, had been assigned to the dozens of Unfallen who, like Cat, had come to live in the safety Sheoul-gra provided to those caught in the gap between Heavenly angel and True Fallen. But footprints on the floor drove Cat nuts, and today, some jackass had tracked in dirt and grass, completely ignoring the new mat she'd placed at the entrance that said, in bold red letters, WIPE YOUR DAMNED FEET.

She thought the play on "damned" was funny, given that almost everyone who came to Sheoul-gra was some sort of demon. Hades had gotten the joke, had laughed when he saw it. She still smiled when she thought about it.

She shot a fleeting glance over at the statue of Seth, which still hadn't been repaired, but at least the two body parts were missing. Maybe Hades was trying to fix them. *Hopefully*, he was trying to fix them.

A tingle of awareness signaled the arrival of a newcomer into the realm – it was kind of cool how anyone who resided in Sheoul-gra developed a sensitivity to the presence of outsiders. It was usually Zhubaal's job to meet visitors, but he was busy, so she leaped to her feet.

Happy to toss her cleaning supplies aside for a few minutes and always curious about who was paying a visit, she hoofed it out of Azagoth's mansion to the great courtyard out front, where the portal from outside was glowing within its stone circle.

And there, striding toward her, was a magnificent male with a full head of blond, shoulder-length hair and a regal stance that could only mean he was a higher order of angel. As a lowly Seraphim, she'd rarely seen angels ranking higher than a Throne, but there was no doubt that this male was at the very top. Perhaps even a Principality, one rank below an archangel.

"E-excuse me, sire," she said, her voice barely a whisper. "Can I help you?"

The big male nodded, his blond mane brushing against the rich sapphire blue shirt that matched his eyes. "I will see Azagoth."

"I'm sorry, but he's busy—"

"*Now.*"

Mouth. Dry. A lifetime of fear of higher angels made her insides quiver, even as she realized that Heavenly angels held no power here. Inhaling deeply, she reached for calm. As a fallen angel in Azagoth's employ, she was actually more influential in Sheoul-gra than this new guy was.

Somehow, that thought didn't make her feel any better.

"This is not your realm, angel," she said sternly. "You can't just poof in here and demand an audience with Azagoth."

"Is that so." The male's voice was calm. Deadly calm. *Scarily* calm.

"Yes. That is so." She was proud of the way her voice didn't quake. Not much, anyway.

A slow smile curved the male's lips, and if it hadn't been so terrifying, it would have been beautiful. "I don't want to cause trouble for you, Cataclysm. So either fetch him or take me to him. Those are your only choices."

"Or?" she asked, and how the hell did he know her name?

Suddenly, the air went still and thick, and massive gold wings sprung from his back, spreading like liquid sunshine far above them both. "Guess."

Holy...*fuck*. He was...he was...a Radiant. An angel who outranked even archangels. And since there could be only one Radiant in existence at any given time, that meant that this was Reaver, brother to Revenant, the King of Hell. That alone would have been enough to terrify her, but making things worse, much worse, was the fact that she had lost her wings because she'd been in league with an angel who had not only betrayed him, but who had attempted to kill his infant grandchild.

Cat's knees gave out, but before she hit the ground, Reaver caught her, landing her on her feet with one arm around her to hold her steady. Instantly, her skin became charged with his Heavenly energy, the magnitude of it rendering her almost breathless.

It was too intense, scattering her thoughts in a way that touching Hades hadn't. As an angel, she'd touched other angels, but it had never been like this. As a fallen angel, she'd had skin-to-skin contact with Lilliana, and while the female had given off a slight positive energy buzz, it hadn't been anything like what she was experiencing with Reaver.

Maybe the fact that she was a fallen angel had made the sensation of goodness too overwhelming for her. Or maybe the intensity had to do with the fact that Reaver was a Radiant. Whatever it was, it made her want to throw up, the way eating too much of a rich food did.

"You okay?" he asked, his voice low and soothing.

She couldn't say a word. But her inability to speak was more than just her reaction to his touch. He was a rock star in the angel world. Beyond a rock star. He was...*the* rock star. *The* angel.

And she'd nearly destroyed his family.

"What the fuck?" Azagoth's voice rang out from somewhere behind her. Dazed, she turned her head to see him walking toward them, his gaze boring into Reaver. "You know that when a high-ranking angel steps foot into my realm, I feel it, right? Like, migraine feel it."

Legs wobbly, she stepped away from Reaver. "Sir—"

A wave of Azagoth's hand silenced her. "I've got this. Reaver is a friend."

"Friend?" Reaver asked, incredulous. "May I remind you that you ordered Hades to hold me in the belly of a giant demon, where I was slowly digested for centuries?"

Cat couldn't believe it when Azagoth rolled his eyes. He wasn't usually so casual with Heavenly angels. But then, Reaver *had* sent gifts for him and Lilliana. "It was three puny months."

"Yeah, well, it felt like centuries," Reaver muttered.

"Good." Now *that* was more like Azagoth. "Are you here to see Lilliana?"

Reaver shook his head. "Unfortunately, I'm here to see you. There's a soul in Sheoul-gra I need to be released."

"Demon?"

"Human."

Azagoth cocked a dark eyebrow. "Really. And why should I do that?"

"Because he shouldn't be there. Your *griminions* took him before his soul could cross over."

"Even if they'd made that mistake, I'd have caught it," Azagoth said, and a knot formed in Cat's stomach.

"You missed this one."

"Impossible."

A bird chirped in the distance, its cheery song so out of place in the growing tension surrounding Azagoth and Reaver. Cat couldn't help but think that the old, lifeless Sheoul-gra might have been a better setting for the confrontation happening right now between these two powerful males.

Reaver stared at Azagoth, his expression darkening with anger. "Seriously? You think Heaven would make that kind of error?"

"You think *I* would?" Azagoth shot back. "In thousands of years, have I ever allowed a non-evil human soul into Sheoul-gra?"

Oh, no. The knot in Cat's belly grew larger as her little incident three days ago filled her thoughts.

"Mistakes happen."

As Azagoth growled, Cat started to sweat. *She* was responsible for the innocent soul being sent into the holding tank. It was the only explanation.

"I don't make mistakes." Azagoth spoke through teeth clenched so hard that Cat swore she heard one or two crack.

"Then someone else did," Reaver said. "I don't give a shit who's at fault. What I do give a shit about is the fact that there's a human soul in the Inner Sanctum who doesn't belong there, and we want him back before he's harmed or someone realizes he's not evil and they use him to break out of Sheoul-gra."

"Um...excuse me," Cat interrupted. "But this person you're talking about...he's a soul, not a physical being, at least not on Earth or in

Sheoul, so how could he be used to help demons escape?"

"Here, as in Heaven, his soul is solid," Reaver said. "A soul-eating demon could absorb him, or his soul could be harvested and liquefied to use in spells." As the horror of what could be happening to an innocent human sunk in, Reaver turned back to Azagoth. "You fucked up big time."

Azagoth snorted. "Bite me."

"You have one week."

"And I repeat—"

"Reaver!" Lilliana's voice rang out, and a moment later, she flung herself into his arms. "It's so good to see you."

They started to chat, giving Cat time to slink away. Holy shit, what had she done? Azagoth had given her a purpose, a home, and safety, and she'd just gotten him into some serious hot water with Heaven.

And that poor human. She'd seen firsthand how traumatic dying could be for humans. Even in Heaven it sometimes took them months to adjust, especially if their deaths were violent or sudden. But to die and then find yourself trapped in hell with no idea why or what you'd done to deserve it?

She shuddered as she shuffled along the stone path toward Azagoth's palace. She had to fix this, but how? Maybe she could find the human herself. Her ability to differentiate between human and demon souls from great distances would be an advantage for her, so maybe, just maybe, she could fix this quickly. If she could get in and out of the Inner Sanctum before anyone noticed she was gone, surely Azagoth would forgive her. It was even possible that the archangels would consider the rescue a good enough deed to allow her back in Heaven.

No one noticed her moving away from the group, so she took the steps two at a time and hurried through the massive doors. The moment she was away from prying eyes, she could no longer maintain her cool composure. She sprinted into action, running so fast through the corridors that she skidded around one corner and nearly collided with the wall on her way to Azagoth's office.

As expected, the office was empty. Terrified, but hopeful that what she was about to do would right a lot of wrongs, she hurried to the lever she'd accidentally opened, the one that had started this whole mess.

Next to the lever that opened the soul tunnel was a switch she'd seen Azagoth and Hades use to gain access to the Inner Sanctum.

When she flipped it, a section of the wall faded out, allowing a view of a dark, shadowy graveyard set amongst blackened, leafless trees on the other side.

For a moment, she hesitated. In Heaven, she'd always been the first of her brothers and sisters to take risks, to step into the unknown. But none of them had ever faced anything like this. To them, taking risks meant speaking up at meetings or chasing a demon into a Harrowgate.

Her two brothers and two sisters would shit themselves if they ever stood where Cat was right now.

The thought gave her a measure of comfort and even made her smile a little. So, before she changed her mind, she took a deep, bracing breath, and stepped through the portal. Instantly, heat so thick and damp she could barely breathe engulfed her. Each breath of fetid air made her gag. The place smelled like rotting corpses. And the sounds...gods, it was as if people in the graves were moaning and clawing at their coffins.

Why would anyone *be* in the coffins?

Fear welled up, a suffocating sensation that seemed to squeeze her entire body. This was a mistake. A horrible mistake. She had to go back. Had to confess what she'd done to Azagoth. Panicked, she spun around so fast she nearly threw herself off balance.

Hurry, her mind screamed. Then it froze mid-scream.

The portal was gone.

Frantic, she searched the wall for a lever of some sort. Or a button. Or a freaking spell that would allow her to use a damned magic word.

"Open sesame?" she croaked.

Nothing.

"Let me out."

Nada.

She pounded on the wall where the door had been. "Open the damned portal!"

The sounds coming from the graves grew louder, and her throat clogged with terror.

She was trapped.

Chapter Five

Cat spent what seemed like forever trying to find a way back to Azagoth's realm, but the solid wall, which reached upward into a pitch-black sky as far as the eye could see, was apparently endless. So was the graveyard. Why was there a graveyard here, anyway?

Even stranger, the headstones, all different sizes, shapes, and materials, were unmarked. At least, they weren't marked with names or dates. Some had been carved with what appeared to be graffiti, and others were scarred by writing, mainly in the universal demon language, Sheoulic. Several were warnings to not enter any of the five mausoleums that seemed to be randomly placed around the sprawling cemetery.

Unfortunately, she'd heard enough about the Inner Sanctum to know that the mausoleums were the gateways to the five levels, or Rings, as they were officially called, that housed the demons Hades watched over. She had to enter. But which one? None were marked in any way that would indicate which Ring they led to. Was she supposed to just choose randomly and hope she'd picked the right one? Ugh. Yet another reason she wanted to go back to Heaven. There, everything was clearly marked.

She eyed the five mausoleums and finally decided on the closest one. Before she entered though, she found a heavy piece of wood she could use as a club if needed. When she'd lost her wings, she'd lost all innate defensive weapons, but they wouldn't have done her any good down here, anyway.

She really should have thought this out a little better.

Your impulsiveness is going to get you in trouble someday.

Her mother's words rang in her ears, and so did her siblings' echoes of, "Told you so," uttered just before her wings had been sliced off.

Cat stared at the mausoleum's iron grate door. Apparently, not even losing her wings had taught her a lesson.

Cursing herself—and throwing in some choice words for her siblings—she pushed open the door, cringing at the rusty creaking noise that made the things in the graves screech. The inside was dark and dusty, but anything was better than the foul dampness of the graveyard. It was also smaller than it appeared to be from the outside, about the size of a phone booth.

The door slammed shut behind her, and she nearly screamed at the clank of the metal hitting the stone. An instant later, it swung open by itself, and she stepped out into a featureless, sandy desert. There was nothing but pale yellow sand and gray sky. Nothing moved. There was no breeze, no sound, no smell...what the hell was this place?

Okay, this might have been a mistake. She spun around to go back to the graveyard and a different mausoleum, but like earlier when she first left Azagoth's library, she found nothing but empty air where the doorway should have been. Panic rose up, but before she could form a coherent thought, she heard a noise behind her. A chill shot up her spine as she slowly turned.

Heart pounding, fingers digging into the wood club, she squinted into the distance, and that's when she saw it—a shimmer in the air that slowly solidified into a number of blurry shapes. And then the shapes took form, and her heart slammed to a sudden, painful stop at the blast of evil that struck her.

At least fifty demons of several different species formed a semicircle around her, a wall of fangs, claws, and crude, handmade weapons. The crowd parted to allow one of them, a seven-foot tall, eyeless thing with tiny, sharp teeth and maggot-colored skin, to come forward. In his slender, clawed hand, he held a chain, and on the other end of that chain, crawling on all fours like a dog, was a human male, his hair matted with blood, his skin bruised and bleeding, one ear missing.

This was the very human she'd come for. Relief quickly gave way to guilt and horror at what had been done to him. And at what might *still* be done to him. To both of them.

"Aren't you a tasty thing," the maggot demon slurred, his voice mushy and sifted through sharp teeth.

Terror, unlike anything she'd ever experienced, clogged her throat.

Oh, she'd been afraid before, plenty of times. But this was different. She'd never faced so many demons, and she'd certainly never done it while holding only a stick of wood as a weapon.

Raising her club, she found her voice, shaky and squeaky as it was. "Demon, I am a fallen angel on a mission from Azagoth himself," she lied. "You are to hand over the human immediately."

Maggot-man laughed. "Foolish *kunsac*." Her Sheoulic was rusty, but she was pretty sure he'd just called her a rather nasty slang term for a demon's anus. "You bluff. And you will die." He grinned, flashing those horrid teeth at her. "But not before we get what we want from you."

Another demon stepped forward and made a sweeping gesture toward the others. "What we *all* want from you."

What they wanted from her? How had they even found her?

They came at her in a rush. She swung her club, catching one in the jaw hard enough to knock a few teeth out, but as she swung again, something struck her in the head. She tasted blood and heard a scream, but only later did she realize that the scream was hers.

* * * *

"My lord."

Inside one of the hundreds of tiny cells in the Rot's lowest dungeon levels, Hades turned away from the broken body of one of the two demons he'd captured three days ago. Silth, the fallen angel commander in charge of the 5th Ring, stood in the doorway. "Tell me you've located the rest of the insurgents."

Silth inclined his blond head in a brief nod. "Yes, but—"

"I trust you've dumped them into the Rot's acid pit?" That was one of Hades's favorite punishments. The demons would splash around as their bodies were dissolved slowly and painfully, until only their souls remained.

That was when things got fun. Exposed souls were delicate, and the acid was even more agonizing on their raw, tender forms. The demons would take another physical body, and then the acid went right back to work, starting the cycle again. It usually didn't take more than a few days before the bastards started talking.

And if that didn't work, dropping them into one of the graves in the cemetery for a couple of decades would.

"Of course." Silth shifted his balance nervously, making his chain mail rattle, and Hades stiffened. "A situation requires your attention."

A dark, slithery sensation unfurled in Hades's gut at both Silth's words and the grim tone. "Tell me."

"The entire 5th Ring is becoming unstable, and the violence is spreading into the 4th Ring. Intelligence indicates that a large-scale escape from Sheoul-gra is in the works."

"Bullshit." Hades kicked at the straw on the floor and watched a hellrat scurry into another filthy pile. "There's no way they could gather enough power to accomplish something like that."

Silth, who Hades had personally chosen as the 5th Ring's warden because he was an evil sonofabitch who liked pain and feared nothing, suddenly looked as if he'd rather be anywhere but here. He even took a step back from Hades, as if he expected to be slaughtered.

Which meant the guy had some fucking bad news.

"Somehow," he growled, "they got hold of an Unfallen."

Hades blinked. "An Unfallen? Like, a living, breathing fallen angel? How? Azagoth wouldn't have allowed anyone inside without telling me." No way. Any living being who was given access to the Inner Sanctum had to be escorted and contained to prevent exactly what appeared to be going on right now in the 5th Ring.

"I saw her myself," Silth said.

"Her?" Hades frowned. "Who?"

"I know not. I caught but a glimpse," Silth said, reverting back to what Hades like to call his "medieval speak." The dude had fallen from Heaven in the late 900's and had spent way too much time messing in human affairs and picking up their annoying habits. "When I captured one of the rebels, he admitted that she was an Unfallen being used in a ritual that would break down the Inner Sanctum's walls."

The hellrat poked its head out of the straw and took a bite out of the unconscious demon on the floor. They were cute little buggers.

"Something's still not right." Hades tore his gaze away from the rodent. "It would take more than a single Unfallen to unleash the kind of magic that would destroy the Inner Sanctum's boundaries. What else do they have?"

"Unknown. But I fear that if we don't act now, it won't matter if the walls fall or not. The uprising is spreading, and if it reaches all of the levels..." He trailed off, knowing full well that Hades understood the seriousness of the situation.

A large-scale rebellion might not result in the destruction of the Inner Sanctum's walls, but it would force Azagoth to halt the admission of new souls into the Inner Sanctum, resulting in a backup that would affect both the human and demon realms. Azagoth had even theorized that a large enough riot could blow out the inner barriers that separated Azagoth's realm from the Inner Sanctum, resulting in a wave of chaos that would destroy everything Azagoth held dear.

Not that Hades gave a shit what Azagoth held dear, but any threat to Azagoth was a threat to Hades, as well. If Azagoth fell, so would Hades, no matter how connected he might be to the Biblical prophecy laid out for Thanatos, the Horseman known as Death.

And I looked, and behold a pale horse; and he who sat on it was named Death, and Hades followed with him.

Yeah. That.

Hades had already helped out the Four Horsemen on several occasions, but he had no idea what was in store for him down the road. No doubt, it wouldn't be good. The Horsemen had a way of getting themselves into trouble.

Hades brushed past Silth and started down the narrow, torch-lit hall, the fallen angel on his flank. "Where are the insurgents holding the Unfallen?"

"My boys and I battled them on the 5th Ring's Broken Claw Mountain." Silth paused as they stopped at the armory, where Hades grabbed a leather harness loaded with blades fashioned from materials found in the Inner Sanctum. Anything from outside was strictly forbidden except inside Hades's home. "The survivors fled into the canyon with the female. I believe they're holed up there."

Hades snorted. "You think they're what, cornered? Waiting to be slaughtered?" Testing the edge of a bone blade, he shook his head. "They have a plan."

"You think it's a trap?"

"Hell, yeah, it's a trap." He grinned because as shitty as the turmoil in the Inner Sanctum was, there was a bright side. Thousands of years of monotony had worn thin, but now there was a little excitement. Something to challenge him, to make him feel alive.

He thought of Cat and how, when she'd run into him in Azagoth's Hall of Souls, he'd had a moment where he'd felt more alive than he had in centuries. It had been enough to make him forget, just for a few minutes, that she was off-limits to him. His pulse had picked up, his body had hardened, and he'd wanted so badly to wrap himself around her and revel in skin-on-skin contact.

But that wasn't going to happen, so he'd have to settle for the next best thing.

A good old-fashioned fight.

Chapter Six

It turned out that Silth hadn't been exaggerating when he'd said that the 5th Ring was in chaos. In the canyon where the Unfallen was supposedly being held, Hades found himself having to fight his way through hordes of demons simply to get within sight of the staging area where the leaders were chanting and dancing and sacrificing demon critters for their blood.

As Hades and his team of fallen angels battled an endless stream of demons, he kept an eye out for the idiot Unfallen who had somehow landed herself in a shit-ton of trouble. Because even if the demons didn't kill her, Hades would.

And he was going to have fun doing it.

He threw out his hand, sending a wave of disruptive power into the crowd of demons in front of him. They blew apart as if they'd been nuked, leaving a path of meat and blood ahead of him. Hellhounds rushed in to feast and snap at the souls rising from the ruined bodies. It wouldn't be long before they reoriented themselves and generated new flesh-and-blood bodies again, so Hades had to hurry. Although only Hades and his fallen angel wardens possessed supernatural powers down here, the demons still had size, strength, teeth, and claws in their arsenals, not to mention sheer numbers. If Hades and his team were overwhelmed, things could get bad. Real bad.

Worse, he'd gone back to his place to contact Azagoth only to find that communications were down, and they must have been for hours. Azagoth always sent a message for a status update at precisely midnight, but for the first time in thousands of years, there was nothing. He probably should have popped into Azagoth's office to see what was up before charging into battle, but dammit, the Grim

Reaper's Darth Vader-ish warning to not fail him again was still sitting on his mind like a bruise, and he didn't feel like poking it. Still, it might have been helpful to know how the hell an Unfallen had gotten into the Inner Sanctum.

Whatever. Regrets were for douchebags.

"There!" Silth pointed to a crude wooden crucifix near the site where animal blood ran thick from a stone outcrop in the cliffs. "The Unfallen."

Hades sprinted toward the crucifix, dodging a volley of spears raining down from demons perched on the rock outcroppings of the canyon's walls. He wished he could use his wings, but flying would make him more of a target. For now, he was safer in the enemy crowd.

He kept his eye on the crucifix as he ran. From this angle, he could make out the slim body of a female hanging limp from the crucifix, arms tied to the cross-board, her head falling forward, her face hidden by a mop of bright red hair. A spark of recognition flared, but it snuffed like a squashed firefly as an axe struck him in the head. Pain screamed through him as shards of bone from his own skull drove into his brain.

"Bastard" he snarled as he wheeled around to his attacker, a burly Ramreel with a black snout and glowing red eyes. "You fucked up my Mohawk." At least, that's what he thought he'd said. The words were garbled. Clearly, the bone shards had also fucked up the part of his brain that controlled speech.

One eye wasn't working, either, but his ability to draw and quarter a demon with a single thought was still intact, as he proved a heartbeat later.

Head throbbing as flesh and bone knit back together, Hades made a run for the Unfallen female. Lightning flashed overhead, and electric heat sizzled over his skin. That lightning wasn't natural. He looked past the giant wooden crucifix, and his hackles raised.

An Orphmage, one of the most powerful sorcerer-class demons that existed, was moving toward the female, a bone staff in his hand. And from the staff, tiny bolts of lightning surged.

Impossible. *Im-fucking-possible.* No one but Azagoth, Hades, and his wardens could wield power here. No one. Not without a source from outside the realm. He supposed the demon could be drawing energy from the Unfallen, but she wouldn't have enough for the kind of magic he was brandishing.

No, something much, much bigger was in play here.

Hades lunged, sending a stream of white-hot electricity at the demon. The Orphmage flipped into the air, avoiding Hades's weapon like he did it all the fucking time. As he landed, he whirled, and in a quick, violent motion, he stabbed the Unfallen in the chest with the sparking end of his staff. She screamed, a sound of such suffering that it somehow drowned out the violence of the battle and reduced the cries of the wounded to muted whispers in the background.

Hades froze. He finally recognized that voice. And that hair. And, as her scream began to fade into a tortured rasp and her body went limp, he recognized her clothes. Faded, torn jeans. Black and emerald corset. Bare feet.

Cat never wore shoes.

The Orphmage stepped back, his head covered by a burlap hood, but Hades could make out a sinister grin stretching his thin lips into a hideous slash. He raised his staff to strike Cat again. With a roar, Hades hurled a series of fireballs at the demon even as he charged toward him. Somehow the demon blocked the fire, but the force of their impacts against his invisible shield still knocked him backward with each blow.

In Hades's peripheral vision he saw one of his wardens go down, his body going one way, his head going another, and dammit, Geist might have been a sadistic tool, but he'd served Hades well for nearly a thousand years.

Quickly, Hades put the dead fallen angel out of his mind and charged up the rocky slope, using his mind to continue throwing shit at the Orphmage. A crude arrow punched through Hades's arm, and as he yanked it out, several more pierced his legs and back. Gritting his teeth against the pain, he hauled himself up the incline and leaped onto the plateau where demons had been making their sacrifices and where Cat was hanging limply from the crucifix.

"Cat," he breathed. "Cat!"

He ran toward her, ignoring the volley of projectiles raining down on him. Pain wracked him, blood stung his eyes, and his battery of powers was draining, but none of that mattered. He had to get to Cat. She was only about thirty yards away, but it felt like he'd run miles by the time he unsheathed a dagger and sliced through the ropes holding her captive.

Awkwardly, he threw her over his shoulder and reached out with his senses to locate the nearest portal. It wasn't far, but naturally, a horde of well-armed, giant demons were standing between him and the way out.

"Hellhounds!" he shouted into the flashing sky. From out of nowhere, two inky canine blurs shot up the side of the canyon toward him. "Make a path!"

Instantly, the hellhound veered toward the group of demons and went through them like bowling balls through pins. Hades followed in the beasts' wakes, reaching the portal as a demon with a missing arm swung a club at him. With relish, Hades sent a blast of power into the bastard's head, exploding it in a fabulous gore-fest.

The portal swallowed him, and an instant later, panting and exhausted, he stepped out of the 5th Ring's mausoleum at the graveyard. He flew the short distance to the wall where portals to and from Azagoth's part of Sheoul-gra were laid out and triggered by only his and Azagoth's voices.

"Open," he barked. Nothing happened. Frowning, he tried again. "Open."

Again, nothing. What the hell? Reaching out, he smoothed his hand over the dark stone surface. It felt the same as always, so why was it not opening?

"Open!" Gods, he might as well have been talking to a wall. He snorted. Sometimes he cracked himself up. "Damn you, fucking *open!*"

Given that the passage was the only way to get out of the Inner Sanctum, this was not good. Had Azagoth sealed the door on purpose? Was this a weird glitch? Or had the demons in the 5th Ring had something to do with this?

Hades wasn't sure which scenario was the better one.

Cat groaned, and shit, he needed to get her someplace safe where she could recover from whatever the Orphmage had done to her. And as soon as she was able to talk, she had some serious explaining to do.

Chapter Seven

Everything was gray. Light gray. Dark gray. And every shade of gray in between.

Cat blinked. Where was she? Squinting, she shifted her head from side to side. She was lying down, apparently inside some sort of lidless stone box. It was huge, about the size of a king-size bed, and like a bed, it had blankets and pillows. Who the hell slept in a giant box?

She sat up, but she was so weak that it took two tries, and as she peered around the room, her head spun.

"Ah, Sleeping Beauty awakens."

Cat turned to the owner of the voice, and she would have gasped if her breath hadn't clogged in her throat. Hades? What was he doing here? Of course, it might help to know where "here" was. "Here" appeared to be a room constructed from the same stone as the box she was sitting in. Iron sconces on the walls gave off a gloomy light, but the fire in the hearth kept the place from being completely horror-movie chic.

"Where am I?" Her voice sounded cobwebby, which seemed appropriate, given that the room looked like a tomb.

"My place." Hades walked over to the far wall where a pot steamed over the fire's roaring flames. He was shirtless today, and the light from the fire flickered over his skin, the shadows defining every glorious muscle as he went down on his heels and ladled something into a cup.

Gods, she was confused. Why was she here? What had happened? The last thing she remembered was being in Azagoth's office...no, wait. She'd gone to the Inner Sanctum to find a human. But everything was pretty cloudy after that.

She rubbed her eyes, which were as blurry as her memories. "What happened to me?"

Hades came over, moving in that way of his, like a panther on the hunt. Not even the chains on his massive black boots made a sound when he walked.

"That's my question for you." He held out the cup, which was really more of a bowl. That looked suspiciously like the top of a skull. "Drink this."

She eyed the contents as she took the bowl, nearly splashing the clear yellow liquid on her hand. It seemed safe enough, wasn't full of floating eyeballs or anything.

"Smells good," she said as she put it to her lips. "What is it?"

"It's a healing broth. Made it myself from the skin and bones of a Croix Viper."

Cat tried not to gag even though the liquid actually tasted decent, like spicy chicken soup. "Thank you." She tried to hand it back, but he shook his head.

"Drink it all. It'll heal the rest of your wounds."

She looked down at herself, but there wasn't a mark on her. Her jeans were dirty, and there were splashes of what might be blood on her feet, but it didn't appear to be hers, and otherwise, she seemed to be in great shape. "What wounds?"

He picked up one of several blades he'd laid out on a crude wooden table and began wiping it down with a rag. "You were pretty messed up when I found you. I have the capacity to heal minor physical damage, but the other stuff is beyond my ability."

"The other stuff?" She watched him slide the blade into a leather harness hanging off a chair.

"Psychic wounds," he said gruffly. "The kind you get when an Orphmage thrusts his magic stick in you."

She drew a sharp breath. "Magic...stick?"

"Not *that* kind of magic stick. Seriously, you ever seen an Orphmage's junk?" He snorted. "I figure they use their staffs to compensate for their tiny dicks."

She'd have laughed if she wasn't so confused about why she was here and what had happened to her. She hadn't spoken to Hades much, but she'd seen how he interacted with others, and she loved his sense of humor. He was so inappropriate and nothing like the people she'd dealt with in her sixty years of life in Heaven. She was pretty sure most angels had *magic sticks* up their asses.

"Maybe I could get out of this..." She looked around at the box she was sitting in. "This...um, coffin? Am I in a freaking coffin?"

"It's actually more of a sarcophagus." He grinned. "Cool, huh?"

Actually, yeah. Hades, guardian of the demon graveyard, had a sarcophagus for a bed. He really lived the part, didn't he?

He offered her his hand, which she took, relishing the hot static buzz that skittered over her skin as she allowed him to help her to her feet and out of the giant coffin. And man, his hand was big. And strong. And it made her wonder what his fingers would feel like as they caressed her skin.

This was the second time they'd touched. She liked it. Wanted more. Being this close to a male was rare and strange, and aside from the unfortunate incident with Zhubaal, she'd never really had more than casual contact with the opposite sex. In Heaven, many angels were all "free-love" and "if it feels good do it," but Seraphim tended to be conservative, determined to use ancient practices like arranged matings in order to preserve the inherent abilities that made Seraphim unique among angels.

She'd always thought Seraphim customs were a drag, even though her parents hadn't been as militant as most others. Even so, just before she'd been booted from Heaven, they'd started to nudge her in the direction of suitable mates.

Now she was on her own, curious, and frankly, she was horny. Her brief encounter with Zhubaal had been ill-conceived and had only left her more sexually frustrated. Although, if she were honest with herself, she could probably lay some of her frustration at her own feet since she hadn't been shy about asking Lilliana about sex with Azagoth.

Lilliana had been shocked at first, but they'd grown close, and soon Azagoth's mate was confiding in Cat, sharing what they did in the shower, with the spanking bench, out in the woods... Cat shivered at the thought of doing some of those things with Hades.

The desire to feel more than the buzz she was getting through their clasped hands became a burning need, and she stepped closer to him, drawn by his bare chest and thick arms. If she could just smooth her palm over his biceps or abs—

Abruptly, he released her and leaped back, almost as if she'd scorched him. A muscle in his jaw twitched as he stood there, staring down his perfectly straight nose as if she were an enemy. And yet...there was an undercurrent of heat flowing behind the ice in his eyes.

Could he read her mind? And if he had, wouldn't her naughty thoughts have made him want to touch her more? She didn't know much about the males of her species, but she knew it didn't take much to get them interested.

"Make yourself comfortable," he said gruffly. "I don't have a lot of visitors, so..." He shrugged as he gestured to one of two chairs in the small space.

Right. So...pretend that neither one of them had been affected by the brief moment of...well, she didn't know what to call it. Maybe avoidance was for the best.

She cleared her throat in hopes of not sounding like a moron. "This is your home? I wouldn't have expected you to live in a one-room...what is this? A crypt?"

"Ding, ding," he said, his voice dripping with sarcasm but not malice. "Give the girl a prize. More snake soup, maybe?"

She held up her still-full bowl. "Thanks, but I'm good." The crackling fire drew her attention to the carved gargoyles on the ends of the mantel and the faded painting of angels battling demons in a cemetery hanging above it. Okay, maybe Hades was taking the graveyard guardian thing a little too far. "So, why do you live in a crypt? Surely you could have a mansion if you wanted."

"You'd think, right?" He gestured to the chair again. "Sit."

It didn't occur to her to not obey, so she sat carefully in the rickety chair that must have been put together by a five-year-old child. As far as she could tell, it was constructed of branches and strips of leather.

Hades folded his arms over his massive chest and stared at her until she squirmed in her highly uncomfortable seat. As if her discomfort was exactly what he was waiting for, he finally spoke.

"Tell me, Cat. What did you do to piss off Azagoth, and why would he send you to the Inner Sanctum without telling me?"

Shit. She was a terrible liar, and she had a feeling that Hades would see through a lie, anyway, but the truth...man, it was probably going to get her punished in a major way. She stalled by sipping the snakey soup.

"Also," he pressed, not missing a beat, "what do you know about communications being down and the door between Azagoth's realm and the Inner Sanctum being locked?"

She choked on the broth. "It's locked for you, too?" At his nod, her mouth went dry. This was bad. Really bad. "I tried to go back, but I couldn't. I thought I screwed something up."

"You screwed up, all right," he said, "but you couldn't have gone back. Only Azagoth or I can operate the doors." He tossed a log on the fire. "Why did you come here?"

Dread made her stomach churn, as if the soup had morphed back into a snake in her belly. "Before I answer your questions, I need to ask something."

"Sure," he drawled, arms still crossed over his chest. "Why the fuck not."

Well, that didn't sound promising. "Azagoth has the ability to destroy souls." She shuddered at the very idea, at the sheer *power* one must possess to undo what God himself had done. "Do you?"

One corner of his perfect mouth tipped up. "You worried?"

"A little."

"Seriously?" He lost the smile. "What the fuck did you do?" His eyes narrowed, becoming shards of angry ice. "Azagoth doesn't know you're here, does he? You entered the Sanctum without his knowledge. Holy shit, Cat, do you know what I'm supposed to do to intruders?"

She could guess, but she really didn't want to. The bowl in her hands started to tremble. *Calm down. He probably won't kill you. Probably.*

"Cat!" he barked. "At least one of my wardens is dead because of you, so I need some answers. *Now.*"

She couldn't look at him, so she concentrated on her feet and said softly, "I accidentally let some souls into the Inner Sanctum."

"Accidentally?"

"Of course it was an accident," she snapped, annoyed that her motives were in question. "Who in their right mind would open the tunnel without Azagoth's permission? I didn't even know *how* to open the thing. I was cleaning, and I accidentally—"

"Okay," he interrupted. "I get it. It was an accident, but that doesn't explain why you're here."

She set the bowl on the edge of the coffin and blew out a breath. "I wanted to fix my mistake. I know it was stupid. I changed my mind, but the portal closed and I couldn't get back."

"So you traveled to the 5th Ring?" he asked, incredulous. "What kind of dumbass move was that? What the fuck were you thinking?"

"I was thinking that I needed to find the human," she shot back, feeling a little defensive. She might be impulsive, and she might not have made the best decision ever, but she had been trying to make things right. "But I swear, I'd barely stepped out when demons surrounded me."

"That's because you're different. You are, for lack of a better word, alive. They can sense your life-force in a way my wardens and I can't." He scowled. "Wait. Human?" He moved a little closer, and she suddenly felt crowded. "What human?"

Ah, yeah, this was where things got really sticky. And bad. "One of the souls that got through...it was human."

"So?" He picked up another of his wicked knives off the table and ran his thumb over the blade. "Evil humans are admitted to the Inner Sanctum every day. The souls you allowed through would have made their way to one of the five Rings...which isn't a catastrophe. Eventually we'd have figured out that they were in the wrong place. *If* they were in the wrong place. So why did you worry about it? Because you were afraid of Azagoth's wrath? Not that you shouldn't be afraid," he threw in. "He peeled me once. *Peeled me.* Do you know what it feels like to be fucking peeled? I'll give you a hint. It's not as fun as it sounds."

Er...she didn't think it sounded fun at all. And geez, she knew Azagoth could be terrifying, but she'd also seen his tender, caring side, and she'd never known him to be needlessly cruel. Then again, by all accounts, Lilliana had softened him considerably. Cat wouldn't have wanted to know Azagoth pre-Lilliana.

"I'm...not sure how to respond to that." But she was sure as hell more afraid of Azagoth than ever. "I mean, yes, I was worried about Azagoth's reaction, but the problem is that the soul was mistakenly brought here. He's human, but not evil. He was reaped by mistake."

"A mistake? How do you know all of this?"

"Because Reaver paid a visit to Azagoth. He wants the human back in a bad way."

Hades went silent, spinning around to pace, his heavy boots striking the floor with great, tomb-shaking cracks. "When did this happen? When did you send the human into my realm?"

She didn't *send* the human into the realm, but she wasn't about to quibble about terminology at the moment. "Three days ago." She reconsidered that, since she didn't know how long she'd been held captive by the demons. "Could be a little longer."

Hades let out a low whistle as he ran his hand over his Mohawk. "Damn, Cat. Just...fuck."

"I know," she said miserably.

"No, you don't know. It all makes sense now. The ritual I came across a few days ago. The Orphmage wielding power. The human was fueling all of it. The damned human is why all of this shit is happening, and with the comms down, Azagoth had no way to warn me."

"What shit?"

"The riots down here. The rebellion." He hurled the knife to the table. The tip of the blade punched into the wood and vibrated, the noise filling the small space with an eerie echo. "The magic."

She shook her head, completely lost. "I don't understand. There have been riots? What magic?"

"The magic that severed communication with Azagoth and sealed the exits out of the Inner Sanctum."

"Sealed? Not just locked? Like, there's nothing you can do?" She couldn't believe that. How could one dead human cause so much trouble? "You're Hades. Surely—"

"No, Cat. That's what I'm trying to tell you. The exit is sealed. We're stuck here, and if the demons are clever enough, they can use the human to reveal the location of my home as well. And once that happens..." He trailed off, and she swallowed. Hard.

She knew she shouldn't ask, but as the psychotic angel she used to work for once said, she was "fatally curious." "Once that happens...what?"

"We'll be overrun by millions of the evilest demons on the Ufelskala scale. They'll kill us, Cat, and if we're lucky, they'll only spend a couple of days doing it."

Chapter Eight

Hades could not believe this shit. In his thousands of years of presiding over the hellhole that was the Inner Sanctum, not a single soul had entered by mistake. Both he and Azagoth had been very careful about who—and what—passed through the barrier. The consequences of the smallest foreign object or unauthorized person entering the Inner Sanctum was precisely why not even his fallen angel wardens were allowed to leave once they started work here. Hades himself couldn't bring anything in, except under certain circumstances, and only with Azagoth's permission.

Made it tough for a guy to get a pizza.

And now, in a matter of days there had been at least two unauthorized entrances, and the full extent of the resulting damage had yet to be seen.

Cat shoved to her bare feet, which were decorated with purple nail polish. Cute. He'd been ordered not to touch her sexually, but would sucking on her toes count?

"So you're saying that we have no recourse?" Her hands formed fists at her sides, and he wondered if she was attempting to keep from punching something. "There's no way to contact Azagoth?"

"I've been trying. My phone has no signal, and even our old methods of communicating through ensorcelled parchment and blood isn't working. I'd been wondering why Azagoth has been so quiet."

"You have a phone down here?" She glanced around as if seeking said device. "A phone that works?"

"I know you haven't been a Heavenly reject for long, but never underestimate the ability of demons to hijack and tweak human advancements." He gestured to a cabinet in the corner. "I have TV, too. Do *not* mess with me on *The Walking Dead* night."

Her delicate, ginger eyebrows cranked down in skepticism. "Are you saying that demons are smarter than humans?

"I'm saying that demons think outside the box and are a lot more creative." He shrugged. "Plus, most of them aren't limited by stifling moral values."

Cat appeared to consider that, her blood-red lips pursing, her pert, freckled nose wrinkling as she thought. "Okay, so we find the human. They must be using his non-evil energy to fuel the spell that cut off the Inner Sanctum from the rest of Sheoul-gra."

He liked that she was thinking this through without freaking out. And as stupid as her decision to enter his realm might have been, he had to admit it was bold—and brave. How many people would have done the same? And how many could have gone through what she had and still be not only mentally intact but willing to keep trying to fix their mistake?

"Maybe," Hades said. "But what did they want with you? Do you know?"

She closed her eyes, her long lashes painting shadows on her pale skin. "I'm not sure. I thought they were going to hurt me, but if they did, I don't remember much of it."

Good, because Hades remembered enough for both of them. Oh, he hadn't witnessed everything that happened to her, but he knew she'd taken a beating at some point. He still couldn't get the bruises and welts that had marked every exposed inch of her body out of his head.

A growl threatened to break free from his throat as he thought about it. Even as he'd laid her carefully in his bed and channeled healing waves into her, he'd sworn to hunt down every one of her attackers and introduce them to his favorite knives.

"Did they say anything to you?" he ground out, still angry at the memory of what had been done to her.

She licked her lips, leaving them glossy and kissable, and he was grateful for something to concentrate on besides her now-healed injuries. "The Orphmage talked about using me to usher in a new world order. Or something crazy like that."

"That sounds about right. Orphmages *are* crazy. But it's a mad scientist kind of crazy that's dangerous as fuck because they can make their insane ideas come to life." Which actually sounded pretty awesome. "Man, if I ever get to be reincarnated, I want to come back as an Orphmage."

"Fallen angels can only be reborn to other fallen angels," she pointed out, as if he didn't know that. "Also, you're twisted."

"Which doesn't stop you from panting after me every time you see me at Azagoth's place." He got a kick out of the way her face went bright red, and he wondered if she was going to deny it.

He wasn't an idiot; he'd seen the way she looked at him. The way she got all flustered when he was near. He loved it. Had come to crave the attention whenever he was visiting Azagoth. He supposed that intentionally seeking her out just so he could get a reaction he couldn't return in kind was a form of self-torture, but hey, torture was what he did, right?

"W-what?" She sputtered with indignation. "I don't do th—"

"You do."

"Don't."

"Do." He laughed. Felt good, but not because he didn't laugh a lot. He just hadn't had a laugh teased out of him by a female in a long time. "It's okay. There's no shame in wanting me. I *am* hot, after all."

She huffed, making her breasts nearly spill out of the tight black and emerald corset she wore. "Whatever," she mumbled. And then she smiled shyly. "I didn't think you noticed."

He nearly swallowed his tongue. He'd been teasing; he hadn't expected her to be bold enough to admit to wanting him. Time to change the subject, and fast, because he wasn't entirely sure he had the willpower to withstand any coy come-ons. He hadn't been with a female in years, not since the last time Azagoth let him out of Sheoulgra. Everyone inside the Gra, including demons, were off-limits to him, and always had been.

That's what you get when you mess with the Grim Reaper's family.

Yeah, he'd brought his punishment on himself, but fuck, he'd made that mistake thousands of years ago. Hadn't he paid his debt by now? He'd asked Azagoth that very question just recently. As it turned out, Azagoth had a long memory, held a grudge, and wasn't the forgiving type.

Shoving thoughts of past mistakes aside, he changed the topic. "So what made you think you could enter the Inner Sanctum and find the human?"

Disappointment at the subject change flashed in Cat's jade eyes, but she covered it with a casual shrug. "I possess a particularly powerful ability to sense good and evil."

"You still have it? Even after you lost your wings?"

She glanced around the room, and instead of answering, she asked, "You got anything to drink? You know, that isn't made from snakes?"

"Sure thing." With a flick of his wrist, the wall behind the TV slid open, revealing a small kitchen that looked like something straight out of *The Flintstones*. Except he had demon-installed electricity. Yay for refrigeration and hot stovetops.

"Huh," Cat said. "I did not expect that. You got a secret bathroom, too?"

"Other wall." As he walked to the kitchen, he heard the wall behind him slide open, heard her murmur of approval.

"Happy to see the shower. Not so happy to see a...what is that, a toilet *trough*?" Her dismayed tone amused him. "That looks like something pigs would eat out of."

"I'm old-fashioned." His amusement veered quickly to shame as he reached into the cupboard for his only two cups. As he plopped them onto the pitted stone counter, he cursed his stark living conditions. They'd never truly bothered him before, but now, seeing how he lived through Cat's eyes had lifted the veil a little, and he didn't like it at all. So instead of going for the rotgut moonshine made right here in the Inner Sanctum, he reached for his prized bottle of rum that Limos, one of the Four Horsemen, had given him three decades ago. "Rum okay? And you haven't answered my question."

"What question? Oh, right. Um, yes, rum is fine, and as far as my ability, it's not as strong as it was before I lost my wings, but I can still feel the difference between good and evil from a greater distance than most haloed angels or True Fallen."

As he splashed a couple of fingers of rum into each cup, he realized that for all of the times he'd seen Cat and asked questions about her during his visits to Azagoth, he knew very little about her. Oh, he'd heard the story of how she fell from grace, how she'd associated with Gethel, the turncoat angel who sold her soul to have Satan's child. He also knew Cat had been brave enough to admit to her mistakes instead of trying to cover them up.

Admirable. Not the route he'd have gone in her situation, but hey, he'd never been a shining beacon of light even when he'd still rocked a halo.

Swiping up the cups, he turned back to her. Damn, she was beautiful, standing in the middle of his living room, barefoot, her jeans ripped in several places, a narrow strip of flat belly peeking between her waistband and her top. But the real showstopper was her hair, that glorious, wavy ginger mane that flowed over her shoulders and breasts in a tangle of wild curls. She looked like a warrior woman plucked from Earth's past, and all she was missing was a sword and shield.

And all he was missing was a brain because those were thoughts he shouldn't be having. He strode back to her and handed her a cup.

"So, with that kind of specialized ability," he began, "what did you do in Heaven?"

"You mean, what did I do before I started working for a traitor who got me booted out of Heaven?" Her voice was light, sarcastic, but there was definitely a bitter note souring the soup.

Of course, if he'd been tricked into nearly starting an apocalypse, he'd be bitter, too.

"Yeah." He raised his sad little bone cup in toast. "That."

She gave him an annoyed look. "I'm a Seraphim. What do you think I did?"

As a Seraphim, who Hades knew was one of the lower angel classes despite what human scholars thought, she would have been required to work closely with humans. "Guardian angel stuff?"

She snorted. "Seraphim don't work in the Earthly realm. We mainly do administrative work for humans who are newly crossed over."

He hoped it wasn't too rude to cringe, because he did. "Sounds boring as shit."

"It is," she admitted. "But because my ability to distinguish good and evil was so strong, my work was a little more interesting."

She was interesting. "How so?"

"Well, all humans are a blend of good and evil, but they're mostly good. They almost immediately cross over to Heaven when their Earthly bodies die." She sank down in the chair again, gingerly, as if it would splinter. It might. Hades had made it himself, discovering in the process that he was a better Lord of Souls than he was Lord of Furniture. "The evil ones are collected by Azagoth's *griminions* and brought here. But if there's any question at all about their level of evil, *griminions* are supposed to leave them alone so they can either remain in the human realm as ghosts or cross over to Heaven on their own. People like that are a very specific mix of equal amounts of good and bad. And others, the ones humans call sociopaths, are even more complicated."

Huh. Hades had never really thought about that. Yes, he knew there were more shades of good and evil than there were stars in the sky, but it never occurred to him that there would be those who walked such a fine line that they would be difficult to place in either Heaven or Sheoul.

"So you worked with the oddballs?"

"We called them Neutrals. Or Shuns." She sipped her rum, her freckled nose wrinkling delicately at that first swallow. "And yes, my job was to feel them out, I guess you'd call it."

He'd like to feel *her* out. It was probably best not to say as much. "How did you do that?"

She smiled and gestured to her bare arms and feet. "Our skin is our power. We can't discern good and evil the way animals, some humans, and other angels do, like a sixth sense. For us, awareness settles on our skin. That's why I cover as little of myself as I can get away with, and what clothes I do wear need to be tight, or sensation can't get through and I feel like I'm suffocating."

Now *that* was interesting. He'd never met anyone who shared his affection for form-fitting clothing. Most people thought tight clothes were binding, but Hades had long ago found that garments that fit like a second skin were more freeing and allowed him to feel the world around him. The air. The heat or cold. The touch of a female...when he could get it.

He took a swig of his rum. "So did you perform your job naked?"

Her eyes caught his, held them boldly, and damn if he didn't stop breathing. He'd been teasing; she was not. "Some of my colleagues did." She reached up and twirled a strand of hair around her finger, and he swore it was almost...playful. "I preferred our standard uniform of what humans would call a tube top and miniskirt."

He pictured that and got instantly hard. But then, he liked her in the ripped jeans and belly-revealing corset she was wearing now, too. He watched her lift the cup to her lips almost in slow motion, watched her throat work as she swallowed.

Damn. He threw back the entire contents of his cup, desperate to get some moisture in his mouth. "And what does good and evil feel like?" he rasped. "On your skin, I mean?"

"I'll show you." She moved toward him, every step popping out her hips and making her breasts bounce in a smooth, seductive rhythm. His mouth went dry again, but then it began to water as she reached out and placed her palm in the center of his chest.

Very slowly, she dragged her hand along the contours of his pecs, her touch so featherlike that he barely felt it, and yet, he was hyper-aware of every move her hand made, every centimeter of skin her palm passed over.

"Goodness and light," she said softly, "is like bathing in Champagne. It's tingly and effervescent. It wakes you up even as it relaxes you."

"Like sex," he murmured. "With someone you like."

"With someone you like?" She blinked. "Why would you have sex with someone you *didn't* like?"

A rumbling purr vibrated his chest. "Baby, it's like fighting, but with orgasms."

"And less blood, I suppose."

"Not if you're doing it right." He waggled his brows, and she rolled her eyes. "So what does evil feel like to you? If good feels good, then does evil feel bad?"

"That's the funny thing." She inched closer, adding another palm to his chest, and he gripped the cup so hard he heard it crack. More. He needed more. And damn her for making him crave it when he'd been perfectly fine being alone for all these years. "It's as seductive as good, but in a different way." She shivered delicately. "It's hot. If good is like bathing in Champagne, evil is like bathing in whiskey. There's a burn, but it's almost always a lovely burn."

Yeah, he felt that lovely burn where she was touching him. As she talked, it spread across his chest and into his abdomen, then lower, to his pelvis and groin. Everything tightened and grew feverish with lust.

"Seems to me," he said in a humiliatingly rough voice, "that bumping up against evil would be an incredible temptation for angels like you."

"It is," she purred. "Which is why we aren't allowed to leave Heaven except under certain circumstances, and even then, we must have an escort. It's one of the reasons I know I can't ever enter Sheoul. To become a True Fallen would be to have my full powers of detection restored, and I'd be skewed toward evil. The few Seraphim who have become fallen angels are like drug addicts, seeking out the most evil beings they can find, to serve them, to just be near them."

He wondered how having a Seraphim fallen angel as a warden in the Inner Sanctum would play out. Then Cat dragged her palms down his chest to his abs, and he forgot all about everything except what was happening right now, right here in his home.

"And what do you feel when you're near me?" He knew he shouldn't ask. Knew he was encouraging something that shouldn't be encouraged, but holy hell, he was starving for female contact. Maybe this little bit would be enough.

And maybe he was lying to himself.

Closing her eyes, she inhaled. "Like I want to climb your body like a tree so you can wrap yourself around me."

Hot...*damn.* He wasn't sure if the rum had gone to her head or if she was affected by his inner evil, but what she'd said made him want desperately to play giant oak for her so she could do whatever she wanted with his hardwood.

Giant oak. Hardwood. Man, he cracked himself up sometimes.

His amusement fled as her fingers brushed his waistband and reality crashed down on him, splintering the tree fantasy. She was clearly not in the right state of mind to understand the consequences of getting physical with him, while he understood far too well.

Cataclysm is off limits to you.

Azagoth's deep voice echoed inside Hades's ears. He'd gone to Azagoth a few months ago, hoping he'd grant Hades permission to see Cat. Hades would have been happy to just talk to her, to get to know her, but Azagoth had been immovable. And then, when Hades had asked Azagoth why, after thousands of years of service, he couldn't even take a walk in Sheoul-gra's lush forests with Cat, the unsatisfying answer had been, *You know why.*

Yeah, he did. *And what if I disobey?*

Do you remember the last time you disobeyed me?

As if Hades could forget. The very memory still made Hades's testicles shrivel. Reluctantly, he stepped back from Cat, but she moved with him, her hands splaying on his torso as they caressed him in slow, sensual circles.

So. Fucking. Good.

Gods, he felt like he'd been deprived of air for so long that he no longer knew how to breathe, and now someone was offering him an oxygen mask but he wasn't allowed to take it.

"Is this really what you want?" He forced the question from his mouth, because dammit, this was really what *he* wanted. He just wanted to take a breath. "To get me worked up?"

"Didn't you just accuse me of panting after you?"

He had. He'd been teasing, but there was nothing funny about this anymore. Her flirtation had been cute and flattering, but it had to stop.

For both of their sakes.

"Yes," he drawled, reaching for the cockiness that had served him well when things got too serious. "But to be fair, all females do."

A slow, seductive smile curved her mouth, and it took a lot more restraint than he cared to admit to keep from dipping his head and kissing her senseless. "I'd tell you that you're arrogant, but I'm sure you already know that. And I like it."

Man, he had no idea how to handle this little vixen. She seemed both innocent and experienced, and he wasn't sure which was the truth.

Maybe it was time to find out.

Chapter Nine

Cat's heart was pounding so hard that she wondered if the surrounding tissue was going to be bruised. After months of trying to catch Hades's eye, she had him all to herself. She had his ear, his eye, and with luck, she'd have him in that coffin-bed.

Yes, there were pressing matters to attend to, but in this moment, they were in background because all she cared about was the foreground. And what a foreground it was.

The problem, she realized, was that she had no idea how to proceed. Things with Zhubaal had gone disastrously wrong, so she didn't want to repeat the mistakes she'd made with him. She just wished she knew what, exactly, she'd done.

Gods, this had better not be a replay of her incident with Z.

Closing her eyes, she let herself feel Hades's unique blend of good and evil on her skin. She'd made the comparison of good feeling like sparkling wine, while evil felt like whiskey, and Hades was a swirling mix of both. Carbonated whiskey. Might taste funky, but her skin felt alive with a tingling heat that spread to her scalp, her toes, and everything in between.

It was especially concentrated in her feminine parts.

So delicious.

"Hades—" She'd barely gotten his name off her tongue when his mouth came down on hers.

"Is this what you want?" he growled against her lips. "I'm not one to question motives when it comes to females who are willing to fuck me, but you have me confused as shit."

She wasn't confused at all. Zhubaal...he'd been an experiment. A means to an end. Oh, she'd liked him, she supposed. He was gruff and rude, but he was never cruel. At least, not that she'd seen.

But Hades was unique. From his clothing to his hair, he blew other fallen angels out of the water. And where most other fallen angels were all serious and dour, Hades was playful, even silly at times. Once, when Thanatos, one of the Four Horsemen of the Apocalypse, had come to Sheoul-gra with his toddler son, she'd watched Hades chase the squealing boy through the courtyard before tackling him gently and then tickling the boy's belly with his Mohawk.

She'd been fascinated to see a legend like Hades, a male whose job it was to make life miserable for millions of demons, handle a child with such tenderness. And he did it with such exuberance, without a care who was watching. How many times had she seen male pride get in the way of fun, as if enjoying life and showing emotion was wrong or weak?

No, it took strength to live the way Hades did and still be able to laugh at a joke or enjoy a child's giggle.

That was the fatal moment in which Cat had decided that she needed to get to know Hades a little better. It was also the moment in which she decided she wanted to feel that blue stripe of hair tickle *her* sensitive spots.

Before she could tell him as much, he spun her, put her hard into the wall, his body against hers. She gasped at the feel of his erection as it pressed into her from her core to her belly. Oh, sweet Heaven, how was that going to feel inside her?

"Most females want me because I'm a monster." He arched against her, and she moaned at the erotic pressure against her sex. "Is that your game? Fuck the underworld's most notorious jailor and earn some bragging points?"

A note of bitterness crept into his voice, but she couldn't tell if he was bitter because of what he was...or if he was bitter because he thought she only wanted him for bragging rights. Either way, it made her want to hug him.

Not long ago, she'd have thought him a monster, but even if she hadn't seen him playing with a child or pilfering bread from Azagoth's kitchen to feed the doves, Lilliana's stories about Azagoth's redemption had touched her. Azagoth had been perched on the precipice of the kind of evil one couldn't come back from, but Lilliana had lured him away from the ledge. Oh, there was still darkness in him—the kind that had made Cat sick for days after accidentally touching him. She had a feeling that if anything ever happened to Lilliana, Azagoth would fall into that black, evil hole and would never return.

But Hades, for all his evil deeds and all the malevolence that surrounded him, had somehow avoided becoming toxic. So, no, he wasn't some sort of fiend, and he wasn't going to convince her otherwise.

She lifted her leg and wrapped it around him, trying to get closer. Trying to get some friction going on. "I don't believe you're a monster."

He scraped his teeth over her ear. "Why not?" he growled, so softly that the crackling flames from the fire nearly drowned him out.

She could have told him the Thanatos story. She could have told him how beautiful he was when he laughed with Lilliana. She could have mentioned the time she saw him smiling as he watched a couple of foxes playing on the edge of the forest just outside Azagoth's mansion. But for some reason, she wanted him to know why her opinion of him was so personal.

"Because I worked with Gethel," she whispered. "She was a traitor who plotted with Pestilence to slaughter a newborn baby and start the Apocalypse."

He brought one hand between them to feather his fingertips across the swell of her breasts, and she went all rubbery in the knees. "So you're saying that in comparison, I'm a saint."

"No." She nipped his lip. "I'm saying you are nuanced. You're evil, but there's good in you, as well."

"You don't know that."

"Expose more of my skin, and I will."

She felt his chest heave against hers. Once. Twice. And then, as if he'd given himself permission, he reached around behind her and ripped her corset off. Thank Heavens she'd chosen the one with the Velcro closure today.

"Now tell me," he breathed into her hair, "do you feel me?"

"Yes," she moaned, undulating her entire body, desperate to get as much skin-on-skin contact as possible. Her nipples, so sensitive they were almost painful, rubbed against the hard planes of his chest. She hadn't known they could ache like that.

"Shit," he rasped. "Too much. This is too much."

Too much what? It wasn't *enough*, as far as she was concerned. "I like touching you."

"No one ever touches me." He took a deep, shuddering breath that somehow sounded...pained, and not in a good way. "Nothing but the wind and rain ever does."

Wind and rain? Was that why he often went bare-chested? He liked the feel of something caressing his skin because people wouldn't? Or maybe he wouldn't let them?

She couldn't imagine living like that. She liked to touch and be touched. To show him how much she enjoyed it, she shoved her hand between them and found his erection as it strained against his pants.

Oh...my. She could feel every ridge and bump through the thin fabric as she ran her fingers along his length. Her strokes, made awkward by her inexperience and their position, still managed to elicit a tortured moan from him. The sound emboldened her, and she gripped him more firmly. His thick length pulsed, the hot blood pounding in her palm, and his shout of pleasure filled the room.

Then, suddenly, he was standing near the portal door and she was slumped against the wall, which was the only thing holding her up. How had he moved so fast? More importantly, *why* had he moved so fast?

"I have to go." For a split second he looked frazzled, his chest heaving, his nostrils flaring. Then he smiled, a cocky lopsided grin that did *not* fit the situation. "Hanging with you was great, but I have people to torture and shit. You can..." He looked around the room. "I don't know. Clean or something."

"*Clean?*" Sure, she was still disoriented from the fog of lust and the surprise of him breaking it all off so quickly, but still...*clean?* "I work for Azagoth. Not you."

He shrugged. "Then sleep. Cook. Watch TV. Whatever. Just don't leave this crypt."

"But I have to find that human."

Reaching behind him, he palmed the symbol carved into the portal door, and it flashed open, turning into a shimmering arch of light. "I'll do it."

She pushed away from the wall, hoping her wobbly legs would hold her up. "I can help."

"No." His tone was harsh, but he softened it as he continued. "The demons were using you for something. Until I know what, we can't risk you being out in the general population. Stay here. I'll be back soon." Before she could protest, he stepped through the portal and disappeared.

"Bastard," she shouted after him.

She swore she heard laughter echo from out of the portal.

* * * *

Lilliana strode through the halls of the building that, just a few short months ago, she'd thought of as her prison. Now it was her home, and the male who ran it was the love of her life.

She found him in his library, standing in front of the fire, his big body outlined by its orange glow. He didn't turn when she entered, even though she knew he'd heard her approach. Coming up behind Azagoth, she wrapped her arms around his waist and pressed her cheek against his broad back.

"Hey."

He covered her hands with his. "My love," he purred. She adored that, how he saved certain tones and words for her and her alone. "What's up? I thought you were busy with the new Unfallen recruits."

"I was, but I couldn't get Cat off my mind."

"Cat? Is she okay?"

She sighed. "I don't know. Have you seen her?"

"Not today." His voice rumbled through her as he spoke. "But I've been busy trying to figure out why Hades won't respond to my messages and why the fucking portals to the Inner Sanctum are sealed."

Yeah, Azagoth hadn't just been busy with that mess—he'd been obsessed. Something was terribly wrong in the Inner Sanctum, and with Heaven breathing down his back over the human stuck inside, Azagoth had been going nonstop. Between researching ways to open the portals and requesting help from the best demon engineers alive, he'd barely had time to eat, let alone sleep.

"You haven't made any progress, I take it?" He made a hellish sound she was going to take as a no. "I'm sorry," she whispered, and that fast, he relaxed a little.

"S'okay." Within the cage of her arms, he turned to her, his gaze intense but concerned. "Now, what's going on with Cat?"

"Did you send her on an errand to the human realm?"

Concern creased his forehead. "No. What's this about? Is she missing?"

"For two days." She stepped away from him, needing room to pace off her nervous energy now that she knew her friend was truly missing. "I didn't worry until today because you sometimes send her off with messages or to fetch things. But she's never been gone this long."

"And you've looked everywhere? The forest? The dorms? The old buildings? You know how she likes to explore."

True. Lilliana had never seen anyone so inquisitive and curious about the world around her. When Cat had first arrived, her constant, prying questions had irked Lilliana until she realized that Cat was simply trying to learn and experience.

"I've scoured all of Sheoul-gra," Lilliana sighed. "I suppose she could be hiding, but there's no reason to do that."

"Maybe she got tired of working here."

She shook her head. "She feels safe here. And even if she did decide to leave, she wouldn't have done it without saying good-bye first." A bad feeling tightened her chest. "Could someone have hurt her?"

He stiffened a little, just a slight shift of his broad shoulders, but Lilliana knew him well enough to recognize genuine unease. "You think one of the Unfallen living here has done something to her?"

God, she hoped not. It had been Lilliana's idea to use the old outer buildings to house Unfallen who didn't want to enter Sheoul, who wanted a chance to make amends for whatever had gotten them booted from Heaven. If one of them had harmed Cat, she'd never forgive herself.

"I don't know," she said. "But I'm telling you, she wouldn't have gone this long without telling one of us. And Sheoul-gra is huge. I searched for her, but there are a lot of places where a person could hide a body or hold someone captive."

Azagoth's eyes went stormy, and Lilliana was very glad the tempest of fury wasn't aimed at her. "If anyone has dared to so much as *touch* a female under my protection," he growled, "I will create a 6th Ring in the Inner Sanctum just for them, and I will fill it with every nightmare they've ever had. They will spend eternity alone, running from the things that scare them most, and just when they think they can't take it anymore, *I* will become the thing they run from."

She shivered. And how twisted was she that she found his threats sexy? Not long ago she'd have thought him a fiend. Okay, he was still a fiend, but only to those who deserved it...and with them, he showed not a shred of mercy. Not even Lilliana would dare get between him and someone he set his vengeful sights on.

So Heaven help anyone who touched Cat, because Azagoth sure as hell wouldn't.

Chapter Ten

Cataclysm spent the next few hours rummaging through Hades's house-crypt. It was probably all kinds of rude to sort through his things, but it was also all kinds of rude to get her worked up and then suddenly back out, tell her to clean his dusty tomb, and then take off. So she didn't feel too bad about snooping through his stuff.

And what interesting stuff it was. Hell, his entire crypt turned out to be a treasure trove of mystery. In addition to the hidden kitchen and bathroom, there was an office, but instead of it being concealed behind a wall, it had been camouflaged by sorcery. His desk, a blocky monstrosity that appeared to have been carved with a pocket knife, sat just inches away from the rickety chair she'd sat in, but she never would have seen it—or bumped into it—if she hadn't picked up the hollowed-out book she found on a shelf. The simple act of opening the book had revealed the hidden desk and file cabinets.

Unfortunately, the cabinets were locked, presumably by more sorcery. But the contents of his desk were more than enough to keep her occupied. She found building plans for an expansion of the 1st Ring, an accounting of the prisoners in some fortress called the Rot, and a list of every fallen angel warden employed in the Inner Sanctum. Then there were the knickknacks on his desktop.

She ran her finger over an egg-sized stone carving of a hellhound, laughing every time she touched its tail because the carving would come to life and snap at her before freezing again in its snarly, crouched stance. Then there was a framed photo of a blue lake nestled between snowcapped mountains. It was beautiful, but why did he have it?

As she went to put it back on the desk, she bumped her elbow, and the picture fell to the floor. Glass shattered, sending shards skidding all over the place.

Shit. Hades was going to kill her.

As she scrambled to clean up the mess, the portal Hades had gone through opened. Of course. Apparently, Hades had the same impeccable timing as Azagoth when it came to her breaking stuff.

"I'm sorr—"

"Who are you?" The deep, unfamiliar voice made her yelp in surprise.

She leaped to her feet, and her surprise veered to terror. A huge male strode into the room, his craggy face shadowed by a filthy, hooded cape that flapped over boiled leather armor as he walked. The necklace of teeth around his neck and the string of ears dangling from the belt around his waist said he was pretty damned comfortable with cutting things off, and she hoped the gore-crusted halberd he carried in one gloved fist wasn't going to be the weapon he used to cut *her* things off.

"W-who are *you*?" she asked, her voice trembling as fiercely as her hands.

As he strode toward her, crusty stuff fell off his boots with every step, and wasn't it crazy that she wanted to yell at him for leaving a mess?

"I'm a warden in the 4th Ring, and you"—he seized her by the throat—"you are an intruder."

"No," she gasped, and then she just tried to breathe because he squeezed harder, cutting off her voice and her air.

His lips peeled back from blackened teeth and a wicked set of fangs as he put his face in hers. "The 4th and 5th Rings are in chaos, and do you know why? There are reports of unauthorized beings in the Inner Sanctum, and it looks like I caught one of them." He grinned, and if she hadn't been struggling to breathe, she'd have screamed. "Do you know what we do to intruders, female? I dare you to imagine the worst because I promise the reality will look far, far more horrible."

His meaty fist filled her vision, and then there was blackness.

* * * *

Hades was balls deep in a demon horde. The 5th Ring had literally been set on fire, and all around, smoke and flame erupted from crude bombs and fire arrows.

He and every 5th Ring warden had been fighting for hours, and they hadn't come any closer to finding the human. Reports of violence were coming in from the 3rd and 4th Rings, as well, and just moments ago, Silth had brought extremely troubling news.

He'd found a weak spot in the membrane that separated the Inner Sanctum from the rest of Sheoul-gra. If the spot wasn't shored up, and fast, demons would overrun Azagoth's realm, which could result in a catastrophic destabilization and allow the souls to escape, flooding human lands.

At least Cat was safely ensconced in his home, although he'd come to realize there was nothing "safe" about her. She might have been an angel once, but he wouldn't be surprised if there was a little succubus in her family tree.

He whacked an ugly-ass demon on its scaly head with his battle-ax and shot a lightning bolt at another. The bolt bounced around the crowd of demons, taking out another dozen before it fizzled away. Shit, this sucked. He'd always liked a good fight, but this was on a scale he hadn't seen since...well, ever.

Panting with exhaustion, he took advantage of the brief reprieve from charging demons. They were all around him, but they were busy fighting wardens, so he figured he had about thirty seconds to breathe.

"My lord!" A towering warden from the 4th Ring powered his way through the crowd and jogged over, his sword dripping with blood. "Malonius sent me with a message. He needs you at the Rot right away."

"Do *not* tell me we're dealing with prison riots, too," Hades growled.

The warden, Rhoni, wiped grime out of his eyes with the back of his gauntleted hand. "No, sir. He captured an intruder."

He frowned. "Someone else was able to get into the Inner Sanctum?"

"Apparently, sir."

Yes. The portals must be operating again. Azagoth must have realized something was wrong and had people working on the problem from his side. Finally. Now he could get Cat back where she belonged.

An uncomfortable sensation caught tight in his chest. He wasn't ready to give her up yet. Sure, he couldn't have her, not in the way he wanted, but now that he'd gotten a taste—so to speak—he wanted more. Her bravery and impulsiveness fascinated him, and her unique blend of artlessness and seductiveness enchanted him. He loved the way her kisses were eager but unpracticed, and her emotions were so unguarded. Such a rare thing for a fallen angel.

Yes, she was newly fallen, and no doubt she'd lose that innocent patina eventually, but only if she was exposed to ugliness. Something inside him wanted to protect her from that ugliness, the way he'd protected humans back when he'd been an angel.

Back then, he'd gone too far in his desire to protect the innocent, and it had cost him his wings and his soul. But how far would he go to protect Cat?

He knew the answer immediately. He'd stop at nothing. Which meant that, if the portals were open, he had to send her back. With only one exception, the Inner Sanctum was ugly, and Cat deserved better. She deserved to not lose her shiny.

The whisper of a spear passed too close to Hades's ear for comfort, jolting him back to the ugliness around him. The kind he needed to protect Cat from.

"How are things in the 4th Ring?" he asked.

"They're bad," Rhoni said, "but not this bad."

Hades clapped the guy on the shoulder. "Get back to it. I'll head to the prison."

Extending his wings, he launched into the air, spinning and diving to avoid projectiles. The icy burn of some sort of weapon ripped through one wing, but a few heartbeats later, he punched through the portal and was striding down the Rot's dark, damp halls to the processing center where all guests were interrogated before being sent to either a cell or a torture chamber. When he arrived in the chilly antechamber, Malonius greeted him.

"She's in Jellybean," he said, his breath visible in the freezing air. "Seems her greatest fear is spiders."

From its pulsating walls to its seeping ceiling, Jellybean was a room that fed on fear and came alive when someone was locked inside. Once it got hold of someone's fears, it made them real. He'd once seen the room fill with jellybeans while the demon inside screamed in terror...hence, the name of the room.

Malonius had shoved an orange bean up the guy's nose, and the demon had confessed all of his considerable sins. *Freaking jellybeans.*

"Wait. She?" Hades asked, every internal alarm clanging as what Malonius said sank in. He opened his mouth, but whatever he was about to say fled when he saw the pile of clothes on the table behind the other fallen angel.

A pair of faded, ripped jeans and a corset.

Cat.

Fuck! Wheeling around, he tore out of the room and charged down the hall, his pulse pounding in his ears even louder than the strike of his boots on the stone floor. Holy hell, if she was hurt, someone was going to pay in blood and bone and pain, and Hades was going to be the one to collect.

Up ahead, a warden stood guard outside Jellybean. "Open that fucking room!" Hades shouted.

The guy jumped, fumbled at his side for the key, but before he could unlock the door, Hades was there. He wrenched the key from the warden's hand and knocked him aside.

His fingers shook as he jammed the heavy iron skeleton key into the lock, but somehow he managed to open the door. He whipped it open, and a wave of spiders of all species and sizes skittered out, spilling over his boots.

"*Dach niek!*"

The Sheoulic command put the room to rest, and the arachnids disappeared. He burst inside, and his knees nearly gave out at the sight of Cat huddled in the corner, naked and shivering. Her arms covered her head as she rocked back and forth on her heels. Bruises marred her pale skin, and fury made his blood steam.

"Cat." He knelt next to her and laid his palm gently on her shoulder, cursing when she flinched. "Cat, it's me. It's Hades."

A shudder wracked her body, and she made a sobbing noise that pricked him in the heart he'd long ago thought immune to pretty much anything emotional.

He lowered his voice, shooting for something that might resemble soothing. "The spiders are gone. They weren't real. It's okay."

Very slowly, her arms came down, and she peeked at him through splayed fingers. Her bloodshot, red-rimmed eyes were a punch in the gut. "Hades?"

"Yeah." He cleared his voice of the hoarseness that had crept into it. "It's okay, I promise."

She lowered her hands, but her gaze shifted and her eyes went wide as the sound of footsteps indicated that someone had come into the room.

"My lord," Malonius began, his voice pitched with fear, proving he wasn't completely stupid. Clearly he realized he'd fucked up in a very, very big way. "I found her in your crypt...she'd ransacked the place...I thought—"

"I know what you thought," Hades snapped. He didn't turn to look at the male because if he did, he wouldn't be able to control the murderous rage pounding through his veins. "And that's the only reason you aren't hanging by your entrails right now."

As much as he wanted to blame the warden for this, it was ultimately Hades's fault. He hadn't thought to tell all of his staff about Cat, but that was a mistake he wouldn't make again.

"Tell the others," he said. "Tell them that this Unfallen is mine, and she's not to be harmed, or ogled, or even fucking *breathed on.*"

"Yes, sir." Malonius tossed Cat's clothes to Hades, and a heartbeat later, they were alone again.

"Cat? I'm going to take you home...ah, I mean, to my place."

He started to pull her into his arms, but he jerked back at the sight of the gore streaking his arms. Cursing, he looked down at himself, realized he must look like he'd showered in a slaughterhouse. The fact that he was covered in blood wasn't the most unusual thing ever, but after what Cat had just been through, she didn't need this, too.

So much for protecting her from the ugliness of the Inner Sanctum.

Guilt churned inside him like a living thing, and this thing had teeth. It gnawed at his heart and clawed at his soul because this could have been prevented.

Cat's teeth began to chatter, so he let the guilt monster feed as he gathered her in his filthy arms and tucked her against his grimy chest and got her out of there, snarling at everyone who got in his way. Or who looked at her naked body. Or breathed in his general direction.

He reached the exit portal in record time, but as he stepped inside, he wondered what else could possibly go wrong.

Chapter Eleven

Face buried against Hades's powerful chest, Cat clung to him with all her strength, which seemed to be in short supply. She couldn't stop the shaking, but when Hades held her tighter and whispered comforting things in her ear, the wonderful whiskey-fizz sensation he gave off wrapped around her like a warm blanket and helped ease the trembling a little.

She didn't open her eyes to see where they were going. She didn't care. As long as she wasn't trapped with spiders in that horrible room with pulsing walls and the faint sound of a heartbeat, she was thrilled. Besides, she trusted Hades. He'd given her no reason not to. More importantly, he worked for Azagoth, and no one in their right minds would do anything to intentionally harm anyone in the Grim Reaper's employ.

Hades let out a hardcore curse, grumbled, and cursed again. She didn't look. Whatever had pissed him off wasn't something she wanted to see. He started moving again, and then suddenly, she felt a cool, fresh breeze on her bare skin. The scent of freshly mown grass and flowers filled her nostrils, and riding on the raft of air was the faint tang of the ocean.

Where in the world were they? Had they escaped the Inner Sanctum?

Still, she didn't peek, not even when he spoke to someone in Sheoulic, dashing her hopes that they'd gotten free. A few moments later, she heard a door close, and the mouthwatering aroma of roasting meat and baking bread finally had her cracking her eyelids.

Her mother had always joked that nothing could make her come running like the ring of the dinner bell, and it was so true. She loved food. Loved to cook. She secretly enjoyed when Azagoth or Lilliana asked her to whip them up something in the kitchen, even though they had several full-time chefs. Sometimes she even helped out in the kitchen that served the dozens of Unfallen who lived and trained in Azagoth's realm.

She wondered how long it would be before she could do that again.

"Where are we?" Her throat, raw from screaming, left her voice shredded.

Holy eight-legged hell, she hated spiders. And, as she'd discovered in that horrible room, demon spiders made every species of arachnid in the human realm seem like cuddly puppies.

"We're with friends. They're letting us take their house for as long as we need." Hades's hand stroked her hair gently. "I'm going to put you down on the bed. Is that okay?"

She nodded, and he set her down carefully on a mattress she suspected had been filled with straw. Before she was even out of his arms, he covered her with a blanket and tossed her clothes onto a small table next to the bed.

They appeared to be in some sort of Tudor-era hut that, while being primitive in comparison to modern-day standards, was pristine, as if brand new. The furniture and decor was simple but elegant and had clearly been fashioned by talented hands. A small, doorless bathroom had been built into one wall, but like Hades's place, the toilet was crude, a mere hole in a stone and wood box she was guessing emptied through some sort of pipe and away from the home.

He sank down beside her on the mattress. "I'm sorry about what happened. I'll be having a little chat with Malonius later."

"Don't," she said, surprising herself. Earlier, she'd cursed that male from here to Mars until she had to stop cursing in order to scream. "He caught me going through your things. I can see why he thought I was an intruder." She shuddered. "The spider room was overkill, though."

"You're a lot more forgiving than most people would be...wait, going through my things?" His voice was teasing and light, so unexpected, and so welcome. How did he know exactly what she needed?

"I was bored. And I wanted to get to know you better." She rolled her bottom lip between her teeth, wondering at what point curiosity became intrusion. "I saw the picture on your desk. The lake in the mountains. Is it someplace special?"

He grunted. "Crater Lake. I've always thought it was one of the most beautiful places in the world, and I need a reminder now and then. Especially since most of the Inner Sanctum is craptastically ugly."

That was so...sweet. And again, unexpected. Who would have thought that the guy who operated a demon holding tank would want something beautiful near him?

"I'm going to go get something for you to eat." Hades reached over and squeezed her hand, but when he glanced down at the way their fingers were entwined, he jerked away from her. "Sorry...I'm covered in...I was fighting before I went to the Rot...fuck." A blush spread over his cheeks as he popped to his feet. "Will you be okay by yourself?"

"I'm not afraid of a little dirt and blood," she said tiredly, "and I'm not a child who can't be left alone." That said, she still checked out the room for spiders. And she couldn't get that infernal heartbeat to stop echoing in her head.

"I know." There was an odd note in his voice...admiration, maybe? The idea that he, a powerful Biblical legend, admired anything about her, a disgraced Unfallen with few survival skills, gave her a boost of much-needed energy. "I'll be right back."

She waited on the bed, the scratchy wool blanket wrapped tightly around her. Soft voices drifted back and forth from the other room, and a few minutes later, he returned with a pottery mug and a bowl of steaming meat and bread swimming in gravy. Her stomach growled fiercely, and she didn't feel the slightest embarrassment when she snatched the plate and crude metal spork from him.

Completely setting aside polite manners, she shoveled a bite into her mouth and chewed. "Oh, damn," she moaned. "This is amazing. But I'm not going to ask what kind of meat it is."

He chuckled as he set the mug on the stand next to the bed. "I can tell you that it's not demon snake."

"Good," she muttered. "I've had enough of that for a lifetime." She took another bite, chewed, swallowed. "So why aren't we at your place?"

"Because Malonius locked the portal to my crypt to protect it, and I can't open it without him. I can break through his lock eventually, but I didn't want to waste time. Besides, I figured you'd be more comfortable here."

She licked gravy off the spork and decided she wanted the recipe.

"Where is here?"

"We're in hell's version of Cloud Cuckoo Land."

"Say what?"

"Don't you watch movies?" He shook his head, making waves in his Mohawk. "We're in a recently-built realm Azagoth and I created for demons who don't really fit into any of the five Rings."

She frowned. "But I thought the Rings coordinated with the Ufelskala."

"They do." He moved over to the window and peered out, his expression watchful but not tense, which relieved her more than she'd care to admit. She'd always thought of herself as being tough, but the last couple of days had tested her resolve, and she was ready for a break. "But the 1st Ring didn't seem suitable for all good demons. There was no reward for demons who have done more than simply exist. Who have contributed to society for the greater good."

As an angel who spent her entire life in Heaven, she'd been raised on stories of the depravity of demons, so while she had no trouble believing that there were demons who were "less evil" than others, she wasn't convinced that "good" demons existed.

"Good demons?" she asked, not bothering to hide her skepticism. "Really?"

He turned away from the window, his big body partially blocking the eerie orange light from outside. "You said yourself that humans come in a wide range of good and evil, so why wouldn't demons? God has always wanted balance, so for every evil human, there exists a good demon."

Cat scooped up a bit of bread and gravy. "Makes sense, I guess. But what kinds of good demons are you talking about?"

The muscles in his shoulders rippled as he shrugged, and her pulse kicked. When she'd clung to him earlier, her lips had been *right there*. She could have kissed him. Licked his skin to see if it tasted as smoky as it smelled.

At least, she could have done all of that if she hadn't been occupied with trying to keep from curling up into a weeping ball of spider-trauma.

"Kinds like the ones who work at Underworld General Hospital." He propped one booted foot against the wall behind him, his pose casual, but deadly energy remained coiled beneath the surface, so tangible that Cat swore she could feel it dance on her skin. He might say they were safe, but he was prepared for anything. So *he* might not feel safe, but she did. Nothing was going to get past him.

"Or the ones who live among humans and do nothing more than try to fit in," he continued. "Before this expansion, they went to the 1st Ring, which is still a pretty hellish experience. Here demons can actually enjoy their time until they're reincarnated. Which, thanks to Revenant being Sheoul's new overlord, happens pretty quickly."

Someone who looked human walked past the window, a ball in his hand. Hades didn't even glance at the guy, but Cat had a feeling he was well aware of every step the male took.

"I'm curious," she said after the guy disappeared. "In Heaven, humans choose their appearance, but everyone can still 'see' each individual as the person they'd always known, even if they knew them on Earth as a twelve-year-old boy, but in Heaven they appear as a twenty-five-year-old female. Is it the same here?"

Hades dipped his head. "Essentially. Demons in the Inner Sanctum do choose their appearances, but people don't always recognize them. I think it's because they're rarely born twice as the same species."

Huh. It hadn't occurred to her that a Seminus demon wouldn't be born again as a Sem. "How does that work?"

He cocked an eyebrow. "Do you really want to talk about this?"

"It's your fault," she said around a mouthful of bread. "You piqued my curiosity."

"Well then," he said with a lopsided grin and an impish glint in his eyes, "I guess I'll have to satisfy your…curiosity."

Oh, yes, please. Satisfy anything you want.

She swallowed about a million times to keep her mouth from opening and those exact words from falling out.

Hades didn't seem to notice the lustful distress he'd caused, continuing his demonic reincarnation lesson as if he hadn't just teased her with sexual undertones. "Demons here are generally reborn as a member of a species that fits within their soul's Ufelskala, but every once in a while a level one will be reincarnated as a species that rates a five, or vice versa. It's why you'll sometimes encounter a Soulshredder that wants to help others, or a Slogthu that likes to kill."

That made sense, she supposed. Anomalies happened in every species on Earth, so why not in Sheoul? "So how does all of this work? How do you keep everyone in line?"

"That's the reason the Rings are all based on the Ufelskala. No matter your score, you can travel to any level that is higher on the scale, but never lower. So an Ufelskala Tier Two demon can travel between the 2nd, 3rd, 4th, and 5th Rings, but they can't go to the 1st Ring. And no one from any Ring can come here."

She considered that for a moment. "But as you said, the Ufelskala scale is based on a species' level of evil as a whole, and not every individual is representative of their breed."

"Which is why Azagoth and my team review every person who comes through the gate." Hades bent over and yanked off his boots. "Now, if you don't mind, I need to clean up."

She scooped up another bite of gravy-soaked bread. "Go for it." Oh, wait...was he going to use the open—*very* open—bathroom? He strode over there, his fingers working at the ties on his pants. Oh, boy, he was going to—

He dropped his pants, and she nearly swallowed her tongue along with the bread. With every silent step, the muscles in his legs and ass flexed, making her fingers curl with the desire to dig into his hard flesh.

Hades hit a lever, and water streamed from a wide slot in the stone wall. He stepped beneath the steaming waterfall, closing his eyes and dipping his head back. He was a living, breathing work of art. Angel and demon all wrapped up in a package of physical perfection. Her mouth watered, but now it had nothing to do with the food. She wanted something much more tasty.

Wanted it desperately. And the thing was, lust had driven her wants before, but something had changed. Yes, when she looked at him, lust was a writhing, burning entity inside her, but there was also a flutter of attraction to the male inside that magnificent body.

But did he want her? He'd spent months avoiding her—or, at least, it seemed that way. And back at his crypt, he'd taken off just when things had gotten hot. But things *had* gotten hot. And he'd sort of flirted a couple times, the way he had a moment ago when he talked about satisfying her…curiosity. So there *was* something there. Right?

She needed to know for sure. Her curiosity had always driven her, even when she should have minded her own business, but a wereleopard couldn't change its spots, could it?

Gathering all her courage, she stood, letting the blanket fall to the floor. His back was turned to her, so he didn't see her moving toward him, her pulse picking up speed with every step.

"Need help washing your back?"

He whirled around, eyes wide, his lips parted in surprise. A blush crept up his neck and into his face as his gaze traveled the length of her body. Between his legs, his sex stirred, swelling and lengthening as he took her in. Between *her* legs, she went wet, and she hadn't even stepped under the water yet.

"I...ah...I'm doing fine by myself..." It was adorable how flustered he was. Big bad Hades was completely off balance. She was so taking advantage of that.

"You missed a few spots." Stepping into him, she gripped his biceps and forced him back around. The tingly, whiskey heat of him immediately sparked on her skin, giving her that contact high that had been so incredibly seductive back at his crypt.

She soaked up the sensation as she palmed the hard bar of handmade soap and began to wash him, starting on the back of his neck and working her way down. Damn, his body was firm, his skin smooth. She'd never touched a male like this, and she made a mental note to do it again. Hopefully with Hades.

Intrigued by this new experience, she committed everything to memory, like the way his muscles leaped under her touch. Like the way the water and suds sluiced over hard flesh that rolled with every one of his rapid breaths. Like the way his fingers dug into the stone wall as if he was trying desperately to hold himself upright.

"Cataclysm," he said roughly. "This might not be the best idea."

Pulse fluttering in her veins, she dropped her hands lower, skimming his buttocks as she scrubbed in wide circles.

"Why not?" She hoped her words came off as light and teasing, that the sound of the water hid the tremor of insecurity. What if he rejected her again?

Taking a deep breath, she went lower, so she was gliding the soap over his firm ass and hips.

"Because."

His voice, husky and dripping with male need, made her bold. "That's not a reason," she murmured as she tucked the soap in the crack of his butt and slid her hand downward, her fingers reaching between his legs—

His hand snapped back to grasp her wrist, and then he was turning into her and pushing her back against the wall. "I think," he said, as he pressed his body against hers, "that it's my turn."

Yes! He did want her!

Dipping his head, he captured her mouth as he wrested the soap out of her hand. His kiss was hotter than the water pouring on them, and his hands, oh, sweet hell, his *hands*. They roamed her body with finesse, his touch alternating between light and firm, teasing and let's-do-this-thing serious. Every pass of the soap over her breasts and buttocks made her groan, and when he dropped the bar and dipped his fingers between her legs, she cried out in relief and amazement. She'd never been touched so intimately before, but now she was glad she'd waited. Hell, she'd have happily given up her wings for this one, beautiful moment.

"You like this," he said in a deep, guttural rasp. "I like it too. I shouldn't, but I do."

There was a strange note in his voice, a tortured thread of...regret? Before she could think too hard on that, he did something sinful to her clit, and she nearly came undone. His fingers slid back and forth between her folds, the pressure becoming firmer as her breath came faster. He changed the rhythm every few strokes to rub circles around her sensitive nub or to slide the pads of his fingers past her opening, hitting a sensitive spot she didn't know she had.

"Please," she begged, not even sure what she was begging for. She wanted everything he could possibly do to her, and thanks to Lilliana, Cat knew a *lot* of things were possible.

He smiled as he kissed a path from her mouth to her jaw and down her neck. Arching her back, she let her head fall against the stone wall to give him as much access as he wanted. He grunted in approval and nipped her throat, the tiny sting adding fuel to the fire that was building inside her.

Another pass of his fingers had her panting and pumping her hips into his hand. Then he slipped one inside her. Yes, oh, damn...*yes!*

He worked her for a moment, wringing sighs and moans from her before adding another finger. The burn of her tissue stretching yielded to pleasure within a couple of heartbeats, and she surrendered herself to his masterful play.

His fingers pumped as his thumb circled her clit, and too soon she exploded, her first climax with a male coursing through her body in an uncontrolled free fall. When she still had her wings, she would sometimes climb high into the air, tuck in her wings, and let the fall take her skimming close to mountaintops and deep into canyons. The orgasm Hades gave her was like that. Freeing, life affirming...and dangerous.

She knew herself well enough to know that for her, sex and emotion would be tightly linked. It was a horrible character flaw, one that had the potential to hurt badly. She supposed it was a good thing Zhubaal had rejected her, but now she thought that maybe Hades should have, too.

He brought her down slowly, his touch growing lighter as she became sensitive to every waning sensation.

"You're so beautiful." His smoky voice rumbled through her like a second climax, sparking a new wave of pleasure skimming across her skin. "God, the sounds you make when you come."

"I need to hear you," she said, taking him in her fist. "Let me."

He gasped, his body going rigid as she squeezed his erection. She'd never touched one before; she and Zhubaal hadn't gotten this far. Not even close. The skin was so silky, the shaft textured with veins she wanted to trace with her tongue.

Suddenly, he seized her wrist and shoved her hand away. Confused, she glanced up at him. He didn't meet her gaze as he backed out of there, leaving a trail of puddles on the wood floor. "I have to go."

What the hell?

"Don't do this again." She shut off the water. "Please, Hades. What's wrong?"

Someone knocked on the door, and she swore he jumped a foot in the air. "Who the fuck is it?" he yelled.

"Silth. I have news you're going to want to hear."

The urgency in Silth's voice said the news wasn't good, but Hades seemed relieved. Was he happy for an excuse to get out of the bedroom? "I'll be out in a second." He didn't bother drying off, simply jammed his feet into his pants. He didn't look at her as he said, "In this part of the Inner Sanctum, and only this part, you can clothe yourself in whatever you want, with just a thought. But the second you leave, the clothes will disappear."

Cool, but clothes were the least of her concerns right now. "Can you slow down for a second?" She reached for one of the folded cloths on the shelf next to the shower. "We need to talk."

"Talk," he said sharply, "doesn't seem to be what you want from me." He held up the hand that had, just moments ago, given her so much pleasure. "I gave you what you wanted, didn't I?"

Stung by his sudden, inexplicable anger, she lashed out. "No, you didn't. Not even close. You think I sit around fantasizing about your *hand?*"

Said hand formed a fist at his side. "Sorry to disappoint, babe."

He yanked open the door with so much force that the iron handle broke. "But I'm sure Zhubaal will be happy to give you whatever it is you fantasize about."

"Wow," she said quietly. "I can see where your reputation as a master torturer comes from. You know exactly where to plunge your dagger, don't you?"

He jerked as if she'd struck him, and then he stormed out, leaving her to her fantasies. Which, right at this minute, included smacking Hades in his stubborn, infuriating head.

Chapter Twelve

What the fuck have I done?

Snarling, Hades slammed the bedroom door and strode into the hut's living room, his hard cock pinching in his pants and his regrets piling up with every step.

He never got this moody, but right now he was strung tighter than a vampire stretched on the Rack in the Rot's dungeon. Sexual frustration combined with the anger from the situation with Cat and the bullshit going on in the Inner Sanctum had damned near reached critical levels. He considered himself to be a pretty laid-back, easygoing guy, especially for a fallen angel, but damn, when he was with Cat it was as if he was mining desires and emotions he'd kept buried, and now he'd hit a vein that ran thick with fury and hopelessness.

It had been centuries since he'd last succumbed to the kinds of feelings that usually signaled an impending catastrophic bout of self-destructiveness.

He either wanted to kill something, or he wanted to fuck something...and the latter something was Cat.

Stupid, Hades. It would be so fucking stupid to start a relationship that can't go anywhere, not to mention the fact that Azagoth will break you in half like a wishbone.

Oh, but didn't he already board that stupid train when he made her the brunt of his anger at not being able to make love to her? She hadn't deserved any of that. Then he'd made it worse by bringing up Zhubaal, which had only served to throw jealousy and shame into the toxic mix brewing inside him right now.

He'd hurt her when he'd sworn to protect her. He'd done what he did best; find a soft spot, slip a blade in it, and give it a good twist.

Fucking idiot.

Water dripped down his back, reminding him of how Cat's gentle fingers had caressed him in the shower. He'd felt like a map and she was the explorer looking for interesting places to go. He'd wanted so badly to let her. Her touch was a gift, a connection he hadn't had with anyone since before he fell. Even then, his relationships hadn't been serious. He'd been young and impulsive, and females had been a fun distraction from his crappy job and his priggish, cold parents.

Since his fall, the few females he'd been with had been sexual partners and nothing more. How could they be anything more when the total of his time outside of Sheoul-gra could be measured in hours instead of days?

Gnashing his teeth, he stopped in front of Silth and tried to keep his tone civil. "What is it?"

"We captured the Orphmage who was holding the Unfallen female you rescued," he said, and Hades's heart leaped. Finally. Maybe he would get to kill someone after all.

"He's alive, I take it."

"Yes, sir." Silth fingered the hilt of the sword at his hip, his chain mail armor tinkling softly as he moved. "We have him at the Rot. But I had a chance to interrogate him at the site where we captured him."

"He talked?"

"After I reached into his chest cavity and started breaking off ribs."

"Nice." Hades nodded in approval. "So what did he say? Did you get the human?"

"No, sir. But he did say that when he jammed his staff into the Unfallen, he released an enchantment inside her."

Hades's heart stopped leaping. "Her name is Cat. And what kind of enchantment?"

"The kind that drains her life force."

Oh, fuck. His heart started beating again, but in an erratic, schizy rhythm. "For what purpose?"

"To open holes in the barriers between the Inner Sanctum and Sheoul, as well as the barrier between the Sanctum and Sheoul-gra."

Not unexpected, since demons were always trying to get out of the Inner Sanctum to wreak havoc as ghosts in both Sheoul and on Earth. But they'd been trying to do that for eons, so what made this attempt different?

"I'm still not clear on how that would work," he said. "What role does the human play in this?"

"They're draining him, too. Both the Unfallen, ah, Cat, and the human are timed to drain at the same time."

Hades's gut was starting to churn. "And how much time do we have before this event takes place?"

"Approximately twenty hours. But it could happen sooner if both the human and the Unfallen are beheaded simultaneously. When their souls flee their bodies, perforations will appear in the barriers, and demons will escape."

Holy shitmonkeys. "Find a hellhound," Hades said. "Quickly."

Silth's upper lip peeled back, revealing two shiny fangs. Like pretty much everyone else, he hated hellhounds. "Why must I track down one of those filthy mutts?"

"Because I need a message delivered to their king. Tell the hellhound that we need Cerberus's help. We can use every hellhound they can spare to find the human."

Silth's curse told Hades exactly how he felt about dealing with the beasts. "And if that fails?"

"Then we'll need the hellhounds to patrol the borders. We can't let a single demon escape, let alone millions of them."

And there was no way he could let Cat die.

"There's one other thing, sir."

Of course there was. "What is it?"

"The enchantment inside the Unfallen...it can be used to track her whereabouts."

Mother. Fuck. "She can't be left alone."

"Do you want me to stay with her?"

Oh, hell, no. Silth was a nasty motherfucker, but he was movie-star handsome and had an insatiable sexual appetite. He wasn't getting near Cat, who had shown herself to be very open about her own sexual appetites.

Gods, she was a dream female. Beautiful and kind, if a little reckless, and when it came to being physical, she wasn't shy...and yet, there was that pesky innocence about her that intrigued him.

And made him crazy, as his outburst in the bedroom had proven.

"My lord?" Silth prompted, and Hades realized he'd gotten lost in his thoughts. "Shall I stay with her?"

"No," Hades said quickly. "I've got it for now. Send the message to Cerberus, and then contact me once we have hellhounds searching the Rings. Cat can help look for the human, but I don't want her out there until we have the hounds for protection."

Silth gave a shallow bow and took off, leaving Hades to wonder what to do in the meantime.

One thing was certain, he wasn't going to tell Cat any of this. She'd been through enough already. Now he had to figure out how to stay with her while not giving into his desire for her. Somehow, he had to pretend that being with her was easy, no big deal, when the truth was that being with her without being inside her might be the hardest thing he'd ever done.

Chapter Thirteen

The longer Hades was gone, the angrier Cat got.

Yes, she understood he was handling business. And given the state of...everything, it was probably serious business. But the way he'd backed out of the shower and run out of the room had been insulting. Of course, his insults had been insulting, too.

Was he playing a game with her? Was he getting a good laugh over the Unfallen panting after him while he remained distant? Was she just a toy for his amusement?

Cursing to herself, she finished drying with the rough linen cloth she'd assumed was meant to be a towel, and then she tried out the "thought clothes" Hades had mentioned. Instantly, she was clothed in jeans and a corset identical to the real ones on the bed. Huh. She changed the colors, turning the corset to bright orange and the jeans to black.

Neat.

But maybe she should try something different. Something that would knock Hades off balance. He thought she should go to Zhubaal to get what she wanted, so maybe she should show Hades exactly what he'd be missing.

But what?

If you want to get a male's attention, give him something to look at.

Lilliana had told Cat that while picking out an outfit to distract Azagoth from some sort of bookwork he'd been poring over a few weeks ago. Hours later, if the spring in Azagoth's step had been any indication, Lilliana's choice of clothes had been spot on.

What the hell, Cat thought. She replicated the outfit, going for a red leather miniskirt and a leather bra top, finishing it off with matching stilettos. Looking down at herself, she smiled. Let Hades resist *that.*

As if on cue, he opened the door. But to her frustration, he didn't so much as glance at her as he crossed to the window.

"Silth found the Orphmage." He brushed back the curtains. "It shouldn't be long before he gives up the location of the human."

Great. Terrific. She should probably say something about that, given that she'd kicked off this entire mess when she came to the Inner Sanctum to find the human.

Instead, she opened her mouth, and something else came out. "What is up with you?" she snapped. "I have been flirting my ass off, and you act like I'm trying to sell you stewed maggots."

"Hey," he said with a wave of his hand. "Don't knock stewed maggots. With enough spices and tomatoes—"

"Argh!" She spun away from him, too angry to continue this. And she hoped like hell he didn't notice her nearly break her ankle on these stupid shoes that clearly didn't work to catch his attention. Nothing did. Maybe it was time to give up and stop being pathetic. "Never mind."

A hand clamped down on her shoulder, halting her in her tracks. A heartbeat later, Hades was in front of her, his expression serious. "Trust me, I'm not immune to your...feminine wiles."

"First of all," she said, shrugging away from his touch, "I don't have any wiles. Second, you're a big, fat liar."

"Baby, you're *wearing* fucking *wiles.*" He grabbed her wrist, and before she could resist, he ground his erection into her palm. "And does this feel like I'm immune? Did I look like I was immune when I was in the shower and you were stroking me?"

Holy shit. She stood frozen to the spot, her hand cupping Hades's massive erection. Finally, she looked up at him, her breath catching in her throat at the glow of heat in his eyes.

"I—I don't understand. If you want me, why have you been such a colossal asshat?"

One corner of his mouth twitched in a smile. "Asshat? I like that."

With a huff, she stepped away from him. "It wasn't a compliment."

"Your hand was on my dick. Anything you said would have been a compliment."

How had he gone from being a jerk to being all charming so quickly? "You still haven't answered my question."

"You want the truth?" Reaching up, he ran his hand over his hair and blew out a long, tired breath. "You're off limits to me."

"Off limits?" she asked incredulously. "Says who?"

"Azagoth."

She scowled, searching her brain for a reason Azagoth would say that, but she came up blank. "Why would he tell you I'm off limits?"

"You mean, why would he tell me that when he didn't seem to give a shit that Zhubaal fucked you?"

Ouch. Flustered, she opened her mouth. Shut it. Opened it again. "That's not what—" She cursed. "How did you know about me and Zhubaal? What did he say?"

"He didn't say anything. That bastard is as tight-lipped as a Ghastem."

Seeing how Ghastems had no mouths...yeah. "Then how did you know? And why do I have to keep asking the same question twice?"

He shrugged, his bare shoulder rolling slowly. "Dunno."

She was going to kill him. "How. Did. You. Know?" she ground out.

"*Griminions* love gossip. Those little suckers live for it. When they aren't collecting souls, I'm pretty sure they hold tea and knitting parties or something."

Hmm. Maybe the reason things with Z had been so disastrous made sense now. Because he'd taken her to his chambers, but then he'd refused sex with her. She'd been pissed, but what if the reason for his reluctance was because Azagoth had forbidden him to be with her?

Sighing, she wished away the shoes and padded barefoot to the wooden chair at the end of the bed. "Is he punishing me, do you think? I keep breaking stuff, and I've missed some cobwebs in corners, and once, I even tracked ashes through his library." She sank down on the chair, her stomach churning. "He's going to send me back to the human realm, isn't he?"

She'd be in danger there, defenseless, easy prey for angel-hating demons and True Fallen who made it a sport to drag Unfallen into Sheoul. Even worse, she'd lose Lilliana as a friend. And she'd never see Hades again. At least, not until she died and came back to the Inner Sanctum as a soul waiting to be reincarnated.

Groaning, she rubbed her eyes with the heels of her palms. She could lose everything, and wasn't that a laugh given how little she actually had. Feeling suddenly very vulnerable, she wished herself new clothes that covered everything. She didn't even mind the suffocating feeling of having so much skin hidden. Right now, the clothing was much-needed armor.

"He's not punishing you," Hades said, his gaze fixed somewhere outside.

"How do you know? Obviously I've angered him somehow."

"Trust me, if he was angry with you, you'd know." He shook his head. "No, Cat, this isn't about you. It's about me." Reaching up, he rubbed the back of his neck. "I'm the one he's punishing. All females in Sheoul-gra are off limits to me, including servants and his daughters. And trust me, when the Grim Reaper tells you his daughters are off limits...you listen. I looked at one of them too long, and he impaled me. Big stick right up the ass and out of the top of my skull. I still pucker when I think about it." His tone was light, breezy, as if his pain was no big deal, but when his gaze caught hers, she sucked in a harsh breath at the sadness there. "I want you, Cat, and if all it would cost me was a pointy stick up the ass, I'd pay that price. But it wouldn't stop there. And I don't know what price you'd have to pay, as well."

Stunned by his admission, she just sat there, unsure what to say. All she knew was that Hades wanted her after all, and that should have made her happy, but the only thing it did was make her miserable.

* * * *

So much for playing it cool.

Hades felt like a total jackass. He shouldn't have said anything about his punishment, about wanting Cat, about anything at all. The only way he stayed sane was to let everything slide off him like lava rolled off a Gargantua.

He wondered if the owners of this hut had alcohol stored somewhere. He could use a drink. Or ten.

"Hades?"

He gazed out the window at the lily pad-choked pond out back and braced himself for a bunch of pity. "What?"

"Is that why you live in the Inner Sanctum? Because Azagoth doesn't want you to be tempted or something?"

"Nope." He watched a crowd of people tossing a ball around in a nearby yard. He hated this place. It was too...human. Too bright and cheery. It reminded him that his life was all gloom and doom and asshole demons.

"So you choose to live in the Sanctum? In what's little more than a hovel?"

He turned back to her, drawing a quick, surprised breath at her clothes. While he'd been looking out the window, she'd changed into tights and a long-sleeved, form-fitting T-shirt. There were even socks on her feet. Since her skin was a gauge for good and evil, she must not want to feel those things. She must not want to feel *him.*

Not that he blamed her, but he still felt a pinch of hurt that made his voice sharper than he'd intended. "What, you were expecting a palace?"

She stared. "You live in a crypt and sleep in a coffin. They make these things called beds now."

What a joke. "Azagoth limits my comforts. You know what I miss most about that? Peanut butter. And chocolate. Limos introduced me to them when they first appeared on the human scene, you know? I always raid Azagoth's kitchen while I'm on that side, but usually I fill up on shit like pizza and Doritos."

Cat had been reaching for a miniature wooden arrow on the shelf next to her, but now she froze, her brows cranked down in confusion. "Azagoth won't even let you bring decent food to your place?"

"Oh, he will. He just won't help me get it. I have to call in favors. Or blackmail people. Limos brought me gelato once, but it was melted by the time Azagoth let it through."

Cat gasped. "That's awful."

He laughed. "It was gelato. Hardly a global disaster."

"Azagoth is an asshole," she snapped. He probably shouldn't love that she was angry on his behalf. "Why is he doing all of this to you?"

"Long story."

She picked up the arrow and gently stroked her fingers over the smooth surface. "Well, we don't have much else to do while we're waiting for the Orphmage to give up the human."

He could think of a lot of things they could do. If he wasn't forbidden by Azagoth to do them.

Anger and frustration threatened to boil over. He'd put up with Azagoth's asshattery for thousands of years, but now...now it felt like he was at a crossroads, at a place where he couldn't stand it anymore. Hadn't he paid for his sins for long enough?

Growling to himself, he stormed out of the bedroom and searched the hut for liquor. Soft footsteps followed him, but he ignored Cat as he popped the cork out of a clay jug of what smelled like extremely potent bloodwine.

Cat drifted into his peripheral vision as she checked out the knickknacks on the walls. Demons loved their wood and bone carvings. "So how did you end up here, anyway?"

He chugged a few swallows of the tart bloodwine, relishing the hot tingle as it burned its way down his throat. "You're a fallen angel, too. You know all about dirty laundry."

A wisp of pink swept across her cheeks. "My fall wasn't entirely my fault."

"You're still going with that story, huh?"

Her chin lifted. "It's true. I told you how it happened."

He snorted. "And Seminus demons hate sex."

She snatched the jug from him and took a swig. He had to hide an amused smile when she coughed. "So you own your fall?" she wheezed as she sat down at the kitchen table.

"Yup." He took back the jug. "I fucked up royally." He brought the container to his lips, pausing to say, "You really want to hear this? You want to know how I got here?"

At her nod, he lowered the jug. He hadn't told anyone this. It wasn't that he gave a crap who knew. It was just that he never really talked to anyone. Not about himself or his life. This was new, and he wasn't sure it was a good thing.

Finally, he propped his hip on the table edge. "When I was still an angel, my job was to process new humans arriving in Heaven after they died on Earth. It was boring as shit, and every time someone came through who had been slaughtered by another human, it pissed me off. So I started spending my time in the human realm, stopping sinners before they committed sins."

"Stopping them? How?"

"At first, I caused distractions. Earthquakes, sudden rainstorms, swarms of mosquitoes, whatever it took. Then I came across some vile bastard in the act of raping a young woman. I didn't think, didn't pause. I flash-fried him with a lightning bolt. And the weird thing is, I didn't feel an ounce of guilt. I knew I was going to be punished because, with very few exceptions, angels aren't supposed to kill humans."

He expected her to show some revulsion, but she merely propped her elbows on the table and leaned forward like a kid hearing a bedtime story. "Did you? Get punished, I mean?"

He shook his head. "Nope. Guess no one was paying attention. So the next time I found an evil human committing an atrocity, I whacked him. Damn, it felt good." So. Fucking. Good. "And that's where it all went wrong."

"Ah," she murmured. "You liked to kill."

Damn straight, he had. "It didn't take long before I wasn't just killing evil humans, but bad humans." There was a difference, a very *important* difference. Evil couldn't be repaired. Couldn't be forgiven. But bad could. "I made no distinction between those who were evil and those who were just assholes. I felt the need to punish, and I was made bolder by the fact that I didn't get caught. Not until I went after a son of a bitch who was famous for his torture methods. Turned out that he was Primori."

"Primori are people whose existence is crucial in some way," she mused, and then her eyes shot wide. "Which means he had a Memitim angel to protect him. And all Memitim..."

"Are Azagoth's children," he finished.

"Oh, shit."

"Yeah." He took another healthy swig from the jug. "The Memitim dude came out of nowhere, and we got into a nasty fight that ended with him dead."

"What did you do?"

Despite the fact that this had taken place over five thousand years ago, Hades's gut sank the way it had way back then when he'd realized what he'd done. He'd killed a fellow angel. Nearly killed a Primori. And worse, he hadn't cared all that much. His concern had been for himself, and for thousands of years, nothing had changed.

Until now. Now his greatest concern was making sure Cat was safe. His own fate was unimportant.

"I knew I'd get caught," he said, "so I ran for a while. Lost myself in the human population. But my parents were both professors of Angelic Ethics, and I'd had their teachings drilled into me since birth, so when the angels started closing in, I figured I'd earn points for turning myself in voluntarily." He curled his lip. "Turns out, not so much. I was relieved of my wings, but instead of being given a new name and booted out of Heaven, I was handed over to Azagoth."

At first, he'd thought the archangels's decision to let him keep his name and send him to Azagoth had been done purely to make the Grim Reaper happy, but once the Biblical prophecy tying him to the Four Horsemen appeared, he understood that he was meant for more than just being Azagoth's plaything.

Not that being a Biblical legend had helped him avoid pain. At all.

"Wow." Cat's already pale skin went a shade paler, making her freckles stand out on her nose and cheeks. "I'm shocked that he didn't kill you."

"Azagoth doesn't kill people." Hades reconsidered that. "Mostly. He's a big fan of eternal torment." No, Azagoth didn't take the easy way when it came to revenge. Or justice. He definitely wasn't the forgiving sort. "He needed someone to run the Inner Sanctum, so he gave me wings and power, making me the only Unfallen in history to be able to enter Sheoul without becoming a True Fallen." He smiled bitterly. "But he also made it his mission to make my life a living hell. And for thousands of years, he did."

She sat back in her chair, her lips pursed in thought. "Is your living situation part of that?"

"Yup." He shrugged. "He's only recently started letting me out of the Inner Sanctum for short periods of time. It's only been in the last fifty years or so that he allowed me to have luxuries from the outside if I can get anyone to bring them to me."

"Like the ice cream Limos brought you."

The pity creeping into Cat's voice made his jaw tighten. "Yeah."

"But you said you can go outside now. How often?"

"I've left Sheoul-gra five times in the last hundred years, and it cost me each time." Even when the Four Horsemen had gotten him sprung to help with a massive battle a few years ago, he'd paid dearly despite the fact that he'd fought for the good guys. For that, Azagoth had taken away Hades's only real friend, a demon who had been living in the 1st Ring for two thousand years. Azagoth had reincarnated him, leaving Hades with only his asshole wardens for company.

"So I'm guessing you don't do much dating if you can't leave, huh? You said females in Sheoul-gra are off limits, but what about here in the Inner Sanctum?"

He laughed. But it was a bitter, hard sound, even to his own ears. "Everyone is off limits to me, Cat. My wardens can screw whoever they want in the Inner Sanctum, but me? Remember the peeling thing I told you about? Yeah. Celibacy and me became really fucking intimate."

"You must have been so lonely," she said softly.

He blinked. Lonely? That thought hadn't occurred to him, and he didn't think it would occur to anyone else, either.

Although, now that he thought about it, yeah, there had always been a strange tension inside him that he couldn't identify. That he'd always written off as being sexual in nature. But now that he'd spent time with Cat, it was killing him to know that it was only a matter of time before he lost her company and her soothing touch. Fuck, he couldn't think about it, because if he did, he'd lose it.

Redirecting his thoughts, he flipped back to his default setting of deflection. "I don't know if I was lonely, really, but I was definitely horny."

She muttered something that sounded suspiciously like, "I know the feeling."

A scream from outside jolted them both to their feet. He rushed to the window and signaled for Cat to stay back, out of sight of anyone who might have a ranged weapon.

"What is it?" she asked. "What's going on?"

Awesomeness, that's what. Turning to her, he grinned. "Ever seen *The Lord of the Rings* or *The Hobbit?* You know how the giant eagles always turn up to save the day?"

She jammed her hands on her hips. "Are you going to tell me that big birds are helping to search for the human?"

Outside, people were still screaming. "Better. The hellhounds have arrived."

"Hellhounds eat people," she pointed out.

"Hilarious, right?" He held out his hand. "Come on. I'll introduce you."

"To the hellhounds?"

"Not just the hellhounds," he said, grasping her hand in his. "To the king himself. Let's go say hi to Cerberus."

Chapter Fourteen

Cataclysm had seen a lot of scary shit in her life—most of it in the last few days—but the massive, two-headed beast standing outside, surrounded by hounds that were as large as bison but still half his size, was one of the most intimidating creatures she'd ever come across.

Black as night, with glowing crimson eyes and teeth that would make a shark jealous, Cerberus used one massive paw to rake deep grooves in the grass. Steam rose up from the damaged earth, turning everything around it to ash.

"Hey, buddy," Hades said. "'Sup?"

The two heads snapped at each other before the left one put its ears back and lowered to eye level. A deep, smoky growl curled up from deep in the beast's chest.

Hades turned to her. "He said his brethren are sweeping the Rings for the human, and he apologizes in advance for any accidents."

"Accidents?"

"Most hellhounds hate angels, fallen or otherwise. Ol' Cerb here barely tolerates *me*. So we can expect some casualties among my warden ranks." He picked up a stick and threw it, and two of the hellhounds took off in a blur of black fur. "Also, he didn't really apologize. It was more of a description of how he thinks they'll taste."

She couldn't tell if he was serious or not, and frankly, she didn't want to know.

Cerberus's other head made some snarling noises, and Hades snarled back. The two of them went back and forth, until finally, Hades held up his hand and turned to her again.

"I...uh...I failed to mention something earlier."

She glared at Hades. She hated being kept in the dark about

anything. "Dammit, Hades, what did you not tell me?"

"The Orphmage who captured you is using your life force to fuel the spell that will open the Inner Sanctum's barriers. He did the same thing to the human. Cerberus thinks that if we can get you close enough to the human, you'll be able to detect him. It should also unlock the doors between the Inner Sanctum and Azagoth's realm. Basically, the mutt wants to use you to track the human. Funny, yes? How it's the opposite of in the human realm, when humans use dogs—"

"I get it," she blurted. And criminy, could this situation get any worse? "But I can't believe you were keeping this from me. My life force? Seriously?"

"I'm sorry," he said, but he didn't sound very contrite. "I didn't want to worry you. Especially not after I was such a dick to you earlier."

Well, at least he admitted to being a dick. "I'm not worried," she explained. "I'm mad. We need to be out looking for the human. I have to fix this so the world isn't overrun by demon spirits and so Azagoth won't expel me from Sheoul-gra." She watched the hellhounds grab the stick and start a game of tug-of-war. "And fixing this could go a long way toward earning my way back to Heaven."

Hades's head jerked back as if he'd been slapped. "Why the everloving fuck do you want to go back to people who kicked you to the curb?"

"Heaven is my home," she said simply.

Even with the growls and snarls coming from the hellhounds and the shouts of people yelling at the beasts from a safe distance, Hades's silence was deafening.

Finally, he said quietly, "Seems to me that home is where the people who want you are."

For some reason, his words knocked the breath out of her. "And who would that be?" she asked. "Azagoth? I clean his house. And not very well. Anyone can do that. He's probably going to fire me anyway, once he learns that I was the one who got the human sent here in the first place. Lilliana? I consider her a friend, and I hope she feels the same about me, but she'd be fine without me. The other Unfallen living in the dorms? Sometimes I cook for them. They'd miss my brown butter vanilla bean cake, but aside from that..."

She shrugged as if it was all no big deal, but the realization that she was so insignificant hurt. Making matters worse was her status as an Unfallen. She had no powers, no status, no identity. Maybe she should have entered Sheoul and turned herself into a True Fallen. At least then she'd have wings and power.

But the cost would have been her soul.

Suddenly, Hades's hands came down on her shoulders. "*I* want you, Cat. I want you more than I've wanted anything since I fell."

Her heart pounded with joy, but a blanket of sadness wrapped around it, muffling the happiness. "And what good does that do either of us if Azagoth is so bent on revenge?"

"Cat—"

She pulled away from him. "Don't make things worse. We need to find the human, and I need to get back to Heaven. Can we do that, please? Before all of my life is drained?"

A chill settled in the air, so noticeable that even the hellhounds looked around to see where the cold front was coming from. Cat didn't bother searching.

An icy glaze turned Hades's eyes cloudy and his expression stony. Blue veins rose to the surface of his skin, which had lost a few shades of color, the way it had back at Azagoth's mansion when he'd shown her his wings. A darkness emanated from him, making her skin burn, and it struck her that this was the Hades who came out to play when things went to hell. *This* was the Jailor of the Dead. The Keeper of Souls. The Master of Torture.

"Tell me, Cataclysm." His voice had gone deep, scraping the craggy bottoms of Hell's fiery pits. "How did you get your name?"

Oh, God. *He knew.* Humiliation shrunk her skin. "It doesn't matter. We should go." She spun around. The door to the hut was just a few steps away—

A hellhound blocked the path, drool dripping from its bared teeth. Clearly, Hades wasn't done with this conversation, but she wasn't going to give him the satisfaction of turning around to face him.

"Did you choose your name?" She jumped at the sound of his voice, so close to her right ear that she felt his breath on her lobe.

"You know I didn't," she ground out, her humiliation veering sharply to anger that he'd chosen to go there. But then, he was the Master of Torture, wasn't he? He'd proven earlier that he knew where to strike in order to extract the most pain from a victim, and names could be an extremely sensitive subject for fallen angels.

When an angel lost his or her wings, they usually got to choose their new names. Heck, a fallen angel could rename themselves over and over, although they were never to use their angel names again. . .except inside Sheoul-gra.

But sometimes, the archangels chose a person's fallen angel name. As a punishment, or an insult, or a lesson...whatever their motivations, when they selected a name for a disgraced angel, it forever rendered one unable to refer to oneself as anything but the name the archangels chose. If they'd wanted Cat's new name to be Poopalufagus, she would be compelled to use it. Hell, she couldn't even *speak* her angelic name if she tried...and she had. The name always got clogged in her throat.

"Why did the archangels choose to call you Cataclysm?" His lips grazed her ear as he spoke.

"Because I was a disaster." Her voice cracked, and she hated herself for it. Hated Hades for making her revisit the worst moment of her life. Hated him more for forcing her to confront a truth she wasn't ready to face yet. "I helped nearly end the world, and they wanted to remind me of it forever."

Silence stretched, and she sensed Hades withdraw. When he finally spoke, his voice was back to normal, but somehow, she knew that nothing would be normal ever again.

"And those are the people you want to go home to." He brushed past her and shooed the hound out of the way. As he threw open the door to the hut and gestured for her to enter, he smiled coldly. "Then, by all means, let's not waste any time getting you back there."

* * * *

Hades spent over twelve hours with a pack of ravenous hellhounds and one fiercely silent female as they searched the 5th Ring for the damned human. Granted, he hadn't felt like talking, either, because ultimately, what did he and Cat have to talk about? Her desire to go back to Heaven, to people who saddled her with a name that would haunt her forever? His selfish desire to prevent that?

Ultimately, there was nothing he could do to convince her not to go back to Heaven if she was given the chance. She didn't want to be here, and even if she did, they couldn't be together. Not if Azagoth was still determined to punish him.

He looked over at Cat, who was standing about thirty yards away on a cliff above a river of lava. In the distance, a blackened volcano spewed smoke and steam as reddish-orange veins of molten rock flowed down its sides. She was dressed in her jeans and corset, and when Hades made clear they were going to be dealing with scorching terrain, she'd agreed to wear a pair of boots loaned to her by a the demons whose hut they'd stayed in.

Hellhounds surrounded her, keeping her safe. The demon canines were unabashed killers, but when given something to protect, they took their job seriously. There was nothing on the planet more loyal than a hellhound. There was also nothing more ravenous, as the half-dozen hellhounds tearing apart some hapless demon nearby proved.

Hades signaled to Silth, and the guy jogged over from where he'd been using a divining rod, fashioned from the thighbone of the Orphmage who had captured Cat, to locate the human. The stupid mage had refused to talk, so they'd gone with Plan *B*. Or, as Hades called it, Plan Bone.

"My Lord?" Silth asked as he climbed the jagged lava rock hill to get to him.

"The hounds want to phase us to another region." Which was awesome because Hades hated this one, despised the heat and the smell. The only upside was that few demons lived here. Which made it a potentially great place to store a human. "But I want you and a few hounds to stay."

"You suspect something?"

Hades couldn't put his finger on it, but there was a sense of wrongness here that went beyond simply not liking the area. They hadn't found anything suspicious, but—

"Hades!" Cat came running toward him, hellhounds on her heels. "I think I can feel the human."

One of the hellhounds with her had something in its mouth, and as she drew to a halt in front of Hades, the hound playfully tossed it at her. She caught it, yelped, and dropped it.

"Hey," Hades said, "he likes you. He just gave you the finger." Of some kind of demon.

She gave him a look of disgust. "How can you joke about that? It's not funny."

"Nah," he said. "It kind of is."

"Gross." She kicked at the digit, and the hound snatched it up, swallowing it in short order. She grimaced and then rubbed her arms. "Like I was saying, I'm sensing something nearby. It's a feeling of good, which shouldn't be here, right?"

"In the 5th Ring? No way." His pulse picked up as the idea that they might be close sank in. "It's gotta be the human. Can you narrow it down to a direction?"

She shook her head. "It's weird, like a thread of good woven into a massive evil cloth. There's too much evil around it to get a bead on it."

"Uh...boss?" Silth held up the wobbling divining bone. "Got something."

As Hades watched, the thing went from barely moving to vibrating so intensely that Silth had to use two hands to hold on.

"Shit." Hades wheeled to the hounds. "Call for backup! Now—"

An arrow punched through his chest. Agony tore through him, but as a hail of arrows fell on them, all he could think about was getting Cat to safety. A fierce, protective instinct surged through him as he took her to the ground and covered her with his body while the hellhounds charged an army of demons pouring out of fissures in the ground that hadn't been there a moment ago.

"Son of a bitch!" Silth, pincushioned by a half a dozen arrows, shouted in anger and pain, but he didn't go down. Palming his sword, he leaped into the fray.

"Let me up," Cat yelled against Hades's chest. "The human is close now. If I can get to him—"

"They're trying to draw you out." He held her tight, cocooning them both in his wings as he peeked between hellhound legs. "They need to behead you both simultaneously to open the holes in the barrier."

"*Behead* me?" she screeched. "Maybe you could have shared that little factoid sooner?"

"Maybe," he said, keeping it light to hide how fucking terrified he was for her. "But nah." He signaled to one of the hounds who had arrived at the hut with Cerberus, a scarred son of the hellhound king Hades knew only as Crush. "Take her to the graveyard. If I'm not there in ten minutes, take her back to the hut."

"What?" Cat punched him in the arm and struggled to her feet. "No. I can help!"

He didn't have time for this, but he gripped her shoulders and shook her. "There are thousands of demons coming at us, all with one goal; to behead you."

"But what about you? If you're not there in ten minutes—"

"Then I'm dead." Before she could say another word, he kissed her. Hard. And he poured as much emotion into it as he could. Because whether they won the battle or not, this would be the last kiss they shared.

Quickly, he stepped back and signaled to the hound. A heartbeat later, the beast was gone, and with him, Cat.

Even above the sounds of battle, he heard her scream, "*Noooooo*," as she faded away.

Chapter Fifteen

Cat and the hellhound materialized in the weird graveyard where she'd started this bizarre journey.

Damn Hades! She eyed the mausoleums that corresponded with the five Rings, but even as she zeroed in on the one she'd originally entered that went to the 5th Ring where the battle was going down, the stupid hellhound got in her way. It even snarled at her.

"You're an asshole," she snapped.

It cocked its big head, raised its pointy ears, and looked at her as if it was expecting her to throw a stick or something. Then it burped. And dear God, what had the thing eaten today? She tried not to gag as she turned around and searched the wall for the opening to Azagoth's realm. Yes, she knew it was locked, but it couldn't hurt to try. It wasn't as if she had anything better to do, since clearly, the gassy hellhound wasn't going to let her go back to the 5th Ring.

Hurry, Hades.

His kiss still felt warm on her lips. Her skin still burned from his touch. She missed him, and they'd only been apart for a couple of minutes. What would happen when—and if—she finally got out of here? How could she deal with knowing he was just a doorway away?

Maybe it would be better if she got to go back to Heaven. He wouldn't be a temptation to her anymore. And besides, being accepted back into Heaven meant her family would take her back, right? Her friends would forgive her. She could forget the terrible things they'd said as she'd been dragged to the chopping block.

Traitor.

Satan's whore.

You're no daughter of mine.

You sicken me.

Yes, she could forget. With enough demon bloodwine, anyway.

An electric tingle charged the air, and the hairs on the back of her neck stood up. She pivoted around as Cerberus materialized, his black fur shiny from blood, one of his massive jaws clenched around a broken, bleeding human.

And dangling limply from the second set of jaws was Hades.

Oh, shit! She sprinted to the giant hellhound, who dropped both bodies to the ground. Sinking to her knees, she gathered Hades's lifeless body in her arms.

"Hades? Hades!" She shook him, but there was nothing. He wasn't even breathing. How could this be? How could he be dead? He couldn't be, right?

"He's only mostly dead."

She wrenched her head around to see Azagoth striding toward them, a trail of *griminions* on his heels.

"M-mostly dead?"

"Haven't you ever seen *The Princess Bride?*"

It took her a second to realize he was making a joke. Mr. Serious, the Grim Fucking Reaper, was *joking.*

The opening in the wall must lead to an alternate reality.

The *griminions* gathered up the human and scurried back through the doorway where Lilliana was waiting.

"Come on," she called out. "Leave Hades to Azagoth."

Cat hesitated, and when Azagoth barked out a curt, "Go," some secret, dark part of her rebelled. She'd just spent what was likely days in a hell dimension with a male who wanted her, a male she wanted, and the person who was keeping them apart wanted her to leave.

Screw that.

She held Hades tighter and boldly met Azagoth's gaze. "I'm staying."

Azagoth's eyes glittered, but his voice was calm. "What I'm about to do won't work if I'm not alone with him, so if you want him to live, you'll go."

Lilliana held out her hand. "Trust him."

Swallowing dryly, Cat nodded. Very gently, she eased Hades's head onto the ground, stroked her hand over his hair, and said a silent good-bye.

Why was this so hard?

"Azagoth," she croaked. "The human and I…the demons

enchanted us, and unless it's broken—"

He cut her off with a brisk hand gesture. "Whatever was done to you will lose its power when you leave the Inner Sanctum. So go. *Now.*"

Sensing he'd reached the limits of his patience with her, she reluctantly shoved to her feet. She managed to keep it together until she was inside Azagoth's office. The moment the door closed, she started bawling, and Lilliana pulled her into a hug.

"I'm so glad you're okay," Lilliana said, and was she crying too? "I knew something was wrong days ago, and then when we tried to operate the doorway to the Inner Sanctum and it wouldn't work, we feared the worst." She pulled back just enough to eye Cat, as if making sure it was really her, and then she hugged her again. And yes, she was crying.

"I'm sorry," she murmured into Lilliana's shoulder. "I screwed up, and when I tried to fix it, I only made things worse."

"It's okay," Lilliana said. "We can hash it out later." She wrapped her arm around Cat's shoulders and guided her toward the door. "Let's get you cleaned up and fed. You must be exhausted."

Cat cranked her head around to the closed portal door. "But Hades—"

"There's nothing you can do for him. Azagoth will update us when he can."

Cat wanted to argue, to rail against being led away, but Lilliana was right. "What about the human?" she asked as they walked toward her quarters. "What happened to him?"

"The *griminions* took him to the human realm where he'll be met by angels and escorted to Heaven."

Good. When most humans died, their souls crossed over to the Other Side on their own, but this poor guy had gone through the worst nightmare imaginable, and if anyone deserved a Heavenly escort, it was him. He'd definitely be sent to a Special Care Unit where humans who died as a result of trauma went to allow them time to adjust. Cat had a feeling he'd need an eternity. She just wished she could do more for him.

Cat was so lost in guilt and worry about Hades that she barely noticed when they arrived at her small apartment. The fragrance of her homemade crisp apple potpourri snapped her out of her daze, and she wasted no time in showering off the remains of the Inner Sanctum. She tried not to think about the fact that Hades was part of that. Gone was the smoky scent of him on her skin. Gone was his touch. His kisses.

She tried not to cry again as she dried off and dressed.

When she was finished, Lilliana was waiting with a tray of food and a pot of hot tea.

"Thank you," Cat said as she took a seat. The food looked amazing, but she couldn't eat. Not until she knew Hades was okay. "It's weird to have *you* serve *me*."

"It's what friends do," Lilliana said. "Also, Azagoth sent word that Hades is fine." Cat nearly slid off her chair in relief. "Like he said, Hades was only mostly dead." She grinned. "I've made Azagoth watch *The Princess Bride* about a million times now. He bitches and moans, but he laughs every time."

That was hard to imagine. "What does 'mostly' dead mean?"

"It means that Hades was killed, but *griminions* grabbed his soul and brought it straight to Azagoth." Lilliana shoved a cup of tea at Cat. "If Azagoth can get a soul to a body fast enough, he can sort of...reinstall and jumpstart." At what must have been Cat's expression of amazement, Lilliana nodded. "Yeah, I didn't know about that until today, either." She propped her elbows on the table and leaned in, her amber eyes glowing with curiosity. "So. What's going on between you and Hades?"

Cat wasn't going to bother asking how Lilliana knew. It was probably written all over her face. She stalled for time though, sipping her tea until Lilliana tapped her fingers impatiently on the table.

"Nothing," Cat finally sighed. "There's absolutely nothing going on with Hades." Saying those words made her heart hurt far more than she would ever have suspected.

"Why? Doesn't he share your feelings?"

"That's not the problem." Man, she was tired. She shuffled to the bed and sank down on the edge of the mattress. "The problem is your mate."

Lilliana's hand froze as she reached for a grape on the platter of food. "What do you mean?"

"You should probably ask him." Cat's lids grew heavy, and she felt herself sway. "Why am I so sleepy?"

"The tea." Lilliana helped ease Cat back on the bed. "It's made from Sora root. It'll help you rest."

Rest would be good. Maybe in her dreams she and Hades could finally be together.

* * * *

The thing about dying was that it made a guy think about his life. What he'd done with it. What he could potentially do with it in the future. And as an immortal, Hades's future could be really long. And really lonely.

The thought of living one more day the way he'd lived the last five thousand years made him want to throw up as he prowled the length of his crypt until he swore the soles of his boots cried out for mercy.

Azagoth had left him hours ago with all kinds of assurances that Cat wouldn't be harshly punished for what she'd done. But Azagoth's idea of "harsh" was a lot different from Hades's. Well, not usually, but for Cat, definitely.

Hades just hoped Azagoth hadn't suspected that anything had gone on between them. Technically, Hades hadn't gone against Azagoth's orders, but the Grim Reaper wasn't a fan of technicalities. And if he did anything to punish Cat for what Hades had done, Hades would fight that bastard until he was too dead to fix.

Snarling, Hades threw his fist into the wall. Never, not in his entire life, had he felt this way about a female. Hell, he hadn't felt this way about anything. Oh, he'd always been passionate about meting out justice, but this was a different kind of passion. This was an all-consuming desire to be with someone. To be something better *for* that someone.

He hadn't known Cat for long, but in their brief time together, he'd shared things he'd always kept private. He'd given comfort and had been comforted. He'd wanted, and he'd been wanted back.

She wants to go back to Heaven, idiot.

Yeah, then there was that. The chances of going back were extremely slim, given that in all of angelic existence, only a handful of fallen angels had been offered the opportunity. But just the fact that she wanted to go was troubling.

Oh, he understood. Who would choose to live in the grim darkness of the underworld when they could flit around in light and luxury? But dammit, Cat was wanted down here. Could he make her see that?

Closing his eyes, he braced his forehead on the cool stone wall he'd just punched. Pain wracked him and not just because he'd broken bones in his hand and they were knitting together with agonizing speed. That pain was nothing compared to the ache in his heart.

He needed to be with Cat, but how? He supposed he could try reasoning with Azagoth. Sometimes the guy wasn't completely unbending. Especially now that he had Lilliana. She'd leveled him out, had given him a new perspective on life and relationships.

But would it be enough?

Because one thing was certain. If Hades couldn't have Cat in his life, then Azagoth had saved it for nothing.

Chapter Sixteen

Cat dreamed of Hades.

It was so real, so sexy, that when she woke, she was both heartbroken to find herself alone in bed and turned on by the things they'd done in her dream. She let her hand drift down her stomach, her mind clinging to the images that had played in her head like an erotic movie. She could almost feel the lash of his tongue between her legs as her fingers dipped beneath the fabric of her panties.

Oh, yes. If she couldn't have him right now, in her bed, she could at least—

Someone knocked on the door, and then Lilliana's voice filtered through the thick wood. "Cat? Are you awake?"

Cat groaned. "No."

Lilliana's soft chuckle drifted into the room. "Azagoth wants to see you in his library."

A cold fist of *oh shit* squeezed her heart, and so much for her libido. It was more dead than Hades had been yesterday.

"I'll be right there," she called out.

It took her less than five minutes to dress in a pair of cut-off shorts and a tank top—she wanted as much skin exposed as possible in hopes that she could sense Azagoth's level of anger in the form of evil. Not that knowing would help her any, but it could at least mentally prepare her for disintegration or something.

Gut churning, she hurried to his library, finding it empty. She took a seat in one of the plush leather chairs, and just as she settled in, Azagoth entered.

She trembled uncontrollably as he took a seat. "Hades told me what happened," he said, getting right to it. "I know that letting the unauthorized souls into the Inner Sanctum was an accident. What I don't know is why you didn't tell me when it first happened. We could have prevented all of this."

"I know," she whispered. She tucked her hands between her knees as if that would stop them from shaking. It didn't. "I should have. But I was afraid. I thought I could fix it on my own, but then I got trapped and couldn't get back...it was all a big mistake."

One dark eyebrow shot up. "A *mistake?* It was a colossal fuckup that could have caused destruction on a global scale. And after the recent near-Apocalypse, having millions of demonic spirits loose in the human world would have damned near started another one."

Her eyes burned, and shame in the form of tears ran down her cheeks. "Are you going to kill me?" Or worse, give her a place of honor in his Hall of Souls, where she'd scream forever inside a frozen body. She wasn't going to ask about that, though. No sense in giving him any ideas.

Azagoth gaped. "Kill you? Why would you think I'd kill you?"

Was he kidding? "You're sort of known for not giving second chances. And for disintegrating people who piss you off."

He appeared to consider that. Finally, he nodded. "True. I've never denied that I'm a monster." He jammed a hand through his ebony hair and sat back in the chair, his emerald eyes unreadable as he took her in. "You're a terrible housekeeper, Cat. You're always breaking and misplacing things, and I doubt you even know what a vacuum cleaner is—"

"I'll do better," she swore. "I'll try harder and work longer hours. Please don't—"

"Let me finish," he broke in. "Like I said, you're a terrible housekeeper. But you're an excellent cook. Zhubaal and Lilliana have watched you with the Unfallen, and they both agree that you're also a great teacher. You're eager and enthusiastic, and I don't think I've ever seen anyone try as hard as you do to get things right. It's that quality that led you to fix the mistake you made by letting the human into the Inner Sanctum. I admire your determination, and I like having you around. So no, I won't kill you. Besides," he muttered, "Lilliana would mount my head on a pike if I did that."

Cat sat, stunned. He admired her? Liked having her around? Even more unbelievable, the Grim Reaper was *afraid* of Lilliana. "I—I don't understand. What are you going to do to me?"

"Nothing. I think you've punished yourself far more than I ever could." He smiled, barely, but for him, that was huge. "I can hire someone else to clean if you'd rather do other work in Sheoul-gra. Just let Lilliana know, and she'll arrange it."

Relief flooded her in such a powerful wave that she nearly fell out of her chair. She could barely function as Azagoth came to his feet in a smooth surge. "I'm glad you're back, Cataclysm. Lilliana was inconsolable."

Inconsolable? Warmth joined the flood of relief. Lilliana truly cared about her. Oh, Cat had had friends in Heaven, but no one had worried about her. Okay, sure, they didn't worry because Heaven was a pretty safe place, but even when she'd gone to work with Gethel, no one had expressed concern. When she'd been found guilty of colluding with a traitor in order to start the Apocalypse, her friends and family had been sad, angry, and embarrassed, but to say that they'd been distraught or inconsolable would be a huge overstatement.

"Thank you," she said, her voice thick with emotion. "But before you go, can I ask you something?"

He gave a clipped nod. "Ask."

She cleared her throat, more to buy a little time than to get the sappy emotion out of her voice. "I want something from you." Azagoth cocked a dark eyebrow, and she revised her statement. "I mean, I would like something from you."

"And what's that?"

"Let Hades have some furniture."

Clearly, Azagoth hadn't expected that because the other eyebrow joined the first. "Furniture?"

"He's been sleeping on a hard-ass slab of stone and using scraps of who knows what for other furniture. He made his own playing cards from bits of wood."

"So?"

She shoved to her feet, ready to go toe-to-toe with him over this. Hades deserved as much. "Don't you think he's been punished enough?"

"You know what he did, yes? You know he slaughtered my son?"

"I'm aware," she said gently...but firmly. "I know that must be painful for you. But I'm also aware that he's been paying for that for thousands of years."

Crossing his arms over his broad chest, Azagoth studied her. His green eyes burned right through her, and she wondered what he was searching for. "He wouldn't ask for these things. So why are you?"

"Because it's the right thing to do."

"Is that all?" he asked, and her stomach dropped to her feet. *He knew.*

"I care for him," she admitted. "And he deserves better—"

"Than how I'm treating him?"

Oh, hell, no, she wasn't falling into *that* trap. "Better than how he currently lives."

When Azagoth smiled, she let out the breath she didn't realize she'd been holding. "Fine. He can have whatever he wants for his home."

She almost pointed out that his home was a damned crypt, but she figured that would be pushing it. So for today, she accepted the victory.

But she wasn't done. Hades had fought for her, and now it was time for her to do the same for him.

First, though, she had someone to see.

Chapter Seventeen

"Can I talk to you?"

Cat stood in the doorway of Zhubaal's office in the Unfallen dorms, her stomach churning a little. She really didn't want to be having this conversation, but curiosity had always been her downfall. Like a real cat.

Zhubaal had been gazing out the window at the courtyard below where several Unfallen were playing a game of volleyball, but now he turned to her, his handsome face a mask of indifference. "About what?"

"I want to know why, ah..." Man, this was awkward. "That day, in your chambers..."

Leaning against the windowsill, he crossed his booted feet at the ankles and hooked his thumbs in his jeans' pockets. "You want to know why I refused sex with you."

Her cheeks heated. That had been a seriously humiliating thing. "Yes. Did I do something wrong?"

"You didn't do anything wrong. I had my reasons."

She probably shouldn't ask, but... "Can you tell me those reasons?"

He stood there for a long time, his expression stony, his mouth little more than a grim slash. Finally, when it became clear that he wasn't going to say anything, she shook her head and started to turn away.

"It's okay," she said. "I had no right to ask."

She headed down the hall, made it about ten steps when he said, "I'm waiting for someone."

Oh. She pivoted around to him as he stood just outside his office door. "Someone you know? You have a lover? A mate?"

He averted his gaze, and she realized that in all the months she'd known him, this was the first time he'd shown any vulnerability. "Not exactly."

Not wanting to ruin the moment, she took a few slow, careful steps toward him, approaching the way she might a feral dog. "Did...did Azagoth warn you to stay away from me?"

"No."

That seemed strange, given that he'd read Hades the riot act. "Why not?"

Gaze still locked on the floor, he replied, "Because he knows about my vow."

"What vow?"

"That," he said, his head snapping up, "is none of your business.

Touchy. But now she was curious. What kind of vow? She recalled his interactions with the resident Unfallen and all the visitors to the realm and realized that she'd never once seen Zhubaal with a female.

"Are you gay?"

He snorted. "Hardly."

Come to think of it, she'd never seen him with a male, either. So what was his deal? He was waiting for someone...someone specific? Was his vow—

She inhaled sharply. "You...you're a virgin, aren't you? You rejected me out of honor."

His gaze narrowed, and his lips twisted into a nasty sneer. "Do not confuse my lack of sexual experience with innocence or kindness, and especially not honor. Not when you tried to use me to rid yourself of your own virginity."

"I didn't know. I'm sorry. I'll just go now. But Zhubaal...I hope you find whoever it is you're waiting for."

As she hurried away, she swore she heard a soft, "I hope so, too."

* * * *

Zhubaal watched Cat disappear around a corner, his heart heavy, his body numb. She had been his single moment of weakness, the only one in nearly a century.

It had been ninety-eight years since his beloved angel, Laura, had been cast out of Heaven. Ninety-eight years of searching for her in Sheoul and getting his own Heavenly boot in the ass in the process.

Cat had come to him in a moment of weakness, on a day when he'd despaired that he'd never find Laura. But even as he'd kissed Cat, touched her, started to undress her, Laura had filled his thoughts.

As young angels, he and Laura had made a blood-pact to be each other's firsts, and he'd kept that vow, even after she lost her wings. He'd searched for her, eventually losing his own wings, but still, he remained faithful. And then, even after he discovered that she'd been slaughtered by an angel, he'd held onto that pact like a toddler with his comfy blankie. After all, her soul had been sent to Sheoul-gra, and he'd figured he could find her there, even if he had to get himself killed to do it.

At least they'd have been together in the Inner Sanctum.

But fate had intervened in the form of Azagoth, who had needed a new assistant, which gave Zhubaal access to privileged information about the residents of the Inner Sanctum.

Then fate threw him a curve ball.

He was too late.

Laura had, indeed, been a resident of the Inner Sanctum's 1st Ring. Until Azagoth reincarnated her thirty years ago.

Pain stabbed Zhubaal in the chest. His Laura was out there somewhere. She was a different person with a different name, but she was still his, and he wouldn't break his vow until he found her.

Unfortunately, he was now bound to Azagoth with a vow just as binding as the one he'd made with Laura. He could leave Sheoul-gra, but only for a few hours at a time, which made searching for Laura— or whatever name she went by now— next to impossible. Especially since Azagoth refused to give any specifics regarding her status, her parents, or even her species.

As a fallen angel, she should have been born only to a fallen angel to become either *emim* or *vyrm*, but Z had learned long ago that there were very few rules that couldn't be broken. For all he knew, his Laura could be feeding on offal and lurking in garbage piles as a Slogthu demon.

The big question was whether or not he'd recognize her. Surely their bond had been strong enough that he could see his Laura in whoever she'd become. And if she'd had the rare good luck of retaining her soul-memory, she could remember bits of her previous life. If so, *she* might even be searching for *him*.

Sighing, he went back inside his office, but he didn't feel like working anymore. He wanted to be out in the world, scouring the realms for Laura. He was a fool and he knew it, but dammit, he'd made a vow, and even if he couldn't have the angel he'd fallen in love with, he wasn't going to break the pact with someone he didn't love. He'd hurt Cat, and he felt a little bad about that, but he hadn't loved her. Cat deserved better. Laura deserved better.

He wasn't sure what he deserved, but he knew what he wanted.

He was just losing faith that he'd ever get it.

Chapter Eighteen

Cat spent the next two days plotting ways to convince Azagoth to lighten up on Hades. Lilliana had volunteered to help, and Cat gladly took her up on her offer. The trick, Lilliana said, would be to make him think it was his idea. As Cat had suspected, he could be incredibly thick-skulled when it came to certain things, like offering second chances.

She opened the door to her apartment, intent on paying Lilliana a visit. But instead of facing an empty hall, she found herself standing mere inches away from Hades. Heart pounding with surprise and excitement, she stared.

"Hades," she gasped. God, he looked good, so good he stole her breath. Wearing nothing but form-fitting, color-shifting pants and black boots, he filled the doorway, his massive shoulders nearly touching the doorframe. "What are you doing here? You'll get in trouble—"

He was on her in an instant. His mouth came down on hers as he swept her into his arms, crushing her against him. His hand came up to tangle in her hair, holding her in place for the erotic assault. Forbidden, shivery excitement shot through her, and her core went molten.

"I don't care," he said against her lips. "I need you. I *burn* for you."

She moaned, her heart soaring at his words as he pushed her toward the bed. But as her knees hit the mattress and they both fell onto the soft covers, she wedged her hands between them and pushed him off.

"I can't," she said, and oh, how it hurt to say that. "I can't watch you suffer because of me."

Hades cupped her cheek in his warm palm. "I was going to go to Azagoth first, but I know him. He'll say no."

"All the more reason to not do this." She heard the sound of the plea in her voice, the weakness in the face of Hades's desire. She needed to be stronger, but she wanted him so badly she shook with the force of it.

He leaned forward and brushed his lips across hers in a feathery, tender kiss. "All the more reason to do it. How does that old saying go? Better to seek forgiveness than ask permission from some asshole who's going to tell you no?"

Damn him, this wasn't funny. "Hades—"

"Shh." He silenced her with another kiss. This one deeper. Harder. "Just this once, Cat," he murmured. "I need this to hold onto when I'm alone at night."

She might have argued some more. She might have shoved him away. She might have done a lot of things if he hadn't slid his thick thigh between her legs as he untied her corset and freed her breasts. If he hadn't dipped his head to take one aching nipple into his mouth.

"Hades," she moaned.

He opened his mouth fully over her breast, his hot breath flowing over her skin as he worked the buttons of her jeans. His tongue teased her as he dragged it low, under the swell of her breast before laving attention on the other one.

Against her thigh, she felt his immense arousal pressing into her, a hot, unyielding presence that she'd never felt in the one place she needed it to be. Arching, she twisted so his erection settled between her legs, but her damned jeans and his pants—

As if Hades was thinking the same thing, he reared up and made fast work of removing her pants. "I love that you don't wear shoes," he said, his voice all breathless and needy. "Nothing to catch your jeans on."

He tossed them to the floor, kicked off his boots, and then stripped away his own clothing, leaving him beautifully, gloriously, naked. His cock jutted upward from the plump sac between his legs, the broad head glistening at the tip. Unbidden, her hand reached out, but he seized her wrists and pinned them over her head as he stretched his body over hers.

"Not yet," he said as he nuzzled her neck. "If you touch me, I'm a goner. Embarrassing, but true."

Okay, she'd let him off the hook. For now. But later, she wanted to touch him. Smell him. Taste him. She had a lot to learn, and she was going to use whatever time they had wisely.

"There you go," he murmured. "Relax. Close your eyes. I'll make this good for you."

Relax, huh? It was weird how her body felt wound tight and liquid at the same time. In the dark behind her eyelids, she imagined the expression on his face as he kissed his way down her body.

His tongue circled her navel, and the tightness ramped up a notch. Anticipation made her squirm, but he put a lid on that quick, clamping down on her hips to force her into blissful submission. Her limited ability to move jacked up the intensity of every sensation until she was clawing at the bedspread and silently begging him to make her come.

But no, Hades was indeed a master of torture, and he took his time scooting lower, his tongue trailing along her abdomen and skimming her mound. She jerked upward, her body instinctively following his mouth as he kissed the crease of her leg.

"You okay?" His voice was a deep, sexy growl that sent stabs of pleasure shooting through every nerve ending.

"Uh-huh," was all she could manage.

He chuckled as he spread her legs and settled between them. The brush of his hair against the sensitive skin of her inner thighs made her hiss in pleasure, and then that soft, prickly Mohawk shifted, finding her center. She moaned as Hades bobbed his head up and down between her legs.

"Oh...my," she breathed. "How...naughty."

He nodded, sending a silky caress over her sex. "There is no part of me that can't bring you pleasure," he purred, the vibration adding to the amazing sensations that cascaded over her in an erotic wave.

His hands slid up and down her legs, circling her ankles and tickling her calves as he brushed his hair over her sex in slow, decadent sweeps. Tension built, a writhing knot of need that grew hotter with every erotic bob of his head. She needed more, and he knew because his head came up and his tongue came out and her eyes went wide when she realized what he was about to do.

"Yes, please," she whispered.

With a raw, erotic curse, he spread her with his thumbs and dipped his head. His mouth met her core, engulfing her in heat as his hot breath fanned the flames. She cried out at the first tentative touch of his tongue. The tip flicked whisper-light over her oh-so-ready knot of nerves before he used the flat of his tongue to lick all of her at once, from core to clit.

She fell back with a strangled moan and drove her fingers through his silky hair to hold him there, to keep him doing exactly what he was doing so perfectly. He lapped at her, starting with long, lazy licks before changing up and swirling his tongue between her folds. But when he pushed his tongue inside her and curled it firmly as he pulled back, she bucked so hard he had to pin her with his hands on her thighs so he could do it again.

Relentlessly, he drove his tongue inside her and licked his way back out, over and over, until the steam building up inside her exploded. The orgasm he'd given her in the shower had been amazing, but this...this made her not only see stars, but join them. The supernova of ecstasy sent her hurtling into the heavens—where she'd never felt like this.

The pleasure rolled over her in great waves, and just when she thought it was over, Hades did something with his fingers and tongue that sent her spiraling out of control again. She heard a distant shout...his name. She'd screamed his name...

Somewhere deep inside her it occurred to her that someone might have heard, but as Hades brought her back to Earth with a series of gentle, slow licks, the danger they faced slipped away until all that was left was the big male prowling back up her body, his lips glistening, his eyes smoldering with the promise that there was more to come.

* * * *

Hades had never in his entire life been this turned on. As an angel, he'd had a couple of sex partners, but he'd been overeager and underexperienced. The encounters had been nice, but all these years later, he could barely remember them.

As a fallen angel, he hadn't had much opportunity to get down and dirty, but when he had, he'd taken advantage of it. The rare times when Azagoth allowed him out of Sheoul-gra, he'd hit every succubus he could find, visited every demon pleasure palace he could get to in his allotted time.

He'd learned a few things, for sure, but one thing he'd never learned was to care. To take the time to enjoy a female with not only his body, but his mind and soul. Maybe because he'd always known he couldn't get attached to anyone, so he'd kept his distance, used jokes and a carefree attitude to breeze through a one-hour stand.

But Cat changed all that. She'd wormed her way into his heart like a dire leech, and all he could do was hope she'd drain him.

Bracing himself on his fists, he looked down at her as she lay panting, her face flushed, her lips parted to reveal just a hint of pearly teeth and tiny, pointed fangs. As the tip of his cock prodded her wet opening, she gasped and rolled her hips, inviting him in.

"I've never done this before," she said. There was no shyness, no self-consciousness, just a plain and simple fact that left him speechless for a second.

"But...Zhubaal," he finally blurted.

She shook her head, making her hair shift in shiny red waves on the pale yellow bedspread. "Nothing happened."

Oh, great, so he'd been a jealous jackass for nothing. It was probably a good thing he hadn't given in to his desire to rip Zhubaal's head off and shove it up his ass every time he saw him, too.

Hades looked into her gorgeous, guileless eyes, loving that she was trusting him to be her first. Pride swelled, but close on its heels was shame. This might be the only time they had, and to take the gift of her virginity, knowing they might never again—

"Knock it off." She dug her nails into his shoulder, the little pricks of pain snapping him out of his train of thought. "I can see your mind working, and I know what you're thinking. I'm capable of making my own decisions, and even if we can't be together again, I want to always have this, same as you."

Ah, damn, she was a gift. This was going to be worth anything Azagoth put him through as punishment. Anything.

Reaching between them, he gripped his cock to guide it inside her, but once again, she clawed him. "Wait. I want to..." She trailed off, a burst of pink blooming in her cheeks. "I want to taste you."

At those words, his cock damned near humiliated him. It jerked in his hand, all, *yes, please, and do it now.*

"Okay," he said, proud of how he didn't sound completely strangled with lust, "but only for a second. You've got me way too worked up."

Her cocky grin made him regret agreeing to this as he climbed up her body and kneeled next to her head. He barely had time to push his unruly erection down when she lifted her mouth to it and flicked her tongue over the bead of pre-come at the tip. He hissed at the contact, hissed louder when she did it again.

And then the crazy little angel swallowed his cock from the head to the base and sucked like she'd been born to do this. A sound somewhere between a shout and a bark escaped him as she slid her mouth upward and swirled her tongue around the crown. Holy hell, she was no tentative kitten lapping at a bowl of milk. This was a she-tiger with an appetite for man, and—

He pulled back and squeezed his cock so hard he lost his sight for a heartbeat. A hot climax pulsed in his balls and his shaft, and there was no way he was blowing down her throat. He needed to be skin-on-skin with her, body to body, sex to sex.

For the first orgasm, anyway.

"Not nice," he scolded, but she just gave him a wide-eyed doe look he might have bought if he hadn't just experienced the rabid carnivore she really was.

"I thought I was being *very* nice." She batted her eyes, still playing innocent, which only made his cock throb harder.

Time to teach her a lesson.

In a quick motion, he flipped her onto her belly and dove between her legs again, lifting her hips for prime access as he stabbed his tongue into her dripping sex. She cried out in surprise and pleasure as he licked her, this time not even trying to be gentle. He growled against her core, nibbling and feasting as he ground his cock against the mattress to keep the bastard happy.

Then, just as her cries and breaths signaled that she was on the edge, he rolled her again. Her legs flopped open, spreading that beautiful pink flesh wide for him. He wanted to lick her some more, but the foreplay had set him on fire, and the bed-humping had fanned the flames.

Time to burn.

He positioned himself between her thighs and pushed against her opening. She arched, giving him even more access, and his head slid into her warmth.

"Tight," he groaned. "Ah, damn, you're tight." Her eyes caught his, held them as he pushed in a little more. Like many angels, she didn't seem to have a barrier, but the invasion still couldn't be comfortable. "Does it hurt?"

"No," she breathed. "It just feels...right."

She couldn't have said anything better. Throwing back his head, he thrust deep. At her cry, he panicked, but the expression on her face wasn't pain. It was bliss. She was so ready, so eager, and he was so damned lucky.

He pulled nearly free of her body and slid back in, keeping an eye on her, gauging her reactions in case he hurt or frightened her, but she was gloriously free of inhibition, fear, or discomfort.

"More," she begged. "Don't hold back. I want it *all*."

It was the same strength of character she'd exhibited in the Inner Sanctum, the drive to get what she wanted at all costs, and this time, he was going to give it to her.

Dropping to his elbows, he kissed her as he pumped between her legs, his thrusts growing faster and harder as his climax began to tingle at the base of his spine. The wet slap of their bodies grew more furious as she clung to him, wrapping her legs around his waist with more strength than he'd imagined she had in her entire body.

She met him thrust for thrust, both with her hips and her tongue. He heard the bed banging against the wall and sliding across the floor with the fury of their joining, and shit, he was close, so close that when she came, all he could do was hold on for the ride.

Her sex rippled along his shaft, wringing the climax from him in long bursts that bordered on agony. Sweet, sweet agony. He couldn't think, couldn't see as he came once, then twice, the second sending his entire body into spasms of ecstasy. He filled her, but she filled him, too, with emotion he'd never known.

And as he collapsed on top of her, his skin coated in sweat, his lungs struggling to pull in enough air, he wondered if he should tell her how he felt about her. Would she believe he was capable of love? He hadn't thought so, but what else could explain his inability to stop thinking about her? What else could explain his willingness to disobey Azagoth? Would it be fair to tell her he'd fallen hard for her?

They had, after all, only known each other for a short time. Worse, Azagoth might kill him.

And then, as if just thinking about the male was a curse, the door slammed open. The Grim Reaper burst inside, the whites of his eyes swallowed by inky black, swirly pools. Massive, leathery wings brushed the ceiling, but it was the set of ebony horns sprouting from his forehead and curling over the top of his skull, that filled Hades with dread. Azagoth only took out his horns when he was pissed.

Yep, Hades was dead. And this time, he had a feeling the "mostly" part wouldn't apply.

Chapter Nineteen

This was a nightmare.

Terror winged its way through Cat as Azagoth strode into her little apartment, black horns jutting from the top of his skull. Lilliana had once said that when the horns came out, so did his temper.

Which was bad, considering that he did most of his killing while being perfectly calm. She didn't even want to *try* to imagine what he'd do while seriously pissed off.

She and Hades leaped off the bed, and while she scrambled for a robe, he very coolly pulled on his pants. Azagoth had the decency to avoid looking at her, but his eyes burned holes through Hades. Who, for his part, showed no emotion at all, although he did keep himself between her and Azagoth. It was sweet of him to want to protect her, but she had a feeling he was in far more danger than she was.

"Azagoth." Hades held his hands up in a placatory gesture, but Azagoth kept moving toward them in a slow, predatory gait. "This isn't—"

"Isn't what it looks like?" Azagoth's words, sounding as if they'd been dredged in smoke, were a dare, and Cat hoped Hades didn't take it.

"No," Hades said, standing his ground and looking completely unruffled. "It's exactly what it looks like. But it isn't Cat's fault. *I* came to *her*."

Tugging her robe closed, Cat stepped next to Hades. "Please, Azagoth," she begged, and she'd go to her knees if she had to, "don't punish him. He saved my life."

Azagoth halted a few feet away, clenching and unclenching his fists at his sides. Claws at the tips of his fingers shredded his flesh, and blood began to drip from his hands. "And you felt grateful enough to sleep with him?"

"Of course not. This started before he saved me." Cat immediately realized her mistake when Hades groaned and Azagoth growled. Quickly, she added, "It was all my fault. He kept telling me he couldn't, and I kept...seducing him."

"You expect me to believe that?"

"It's the truth," she said, "so, yes."

Azagoth turned to Hades, and was it her imagination or had his horns receded a little? "And what have you got to say?"

"She's telling the truth. But..."

"But what?"

"But I could have resisted more. I chose not to." He took her hand. "I want her."

"I see." Azagoth scrubbed his palm over his face, leaving behind smears of blood like evil war paint. "Lilliana has made me soft," he muttered. He dropped his hand and studied each of them in turn before focusing his laser gaze on Hades. "Will you fight for her?"

Hades growled. "I would fight Revenant himself for her."

Azagoth's upper lip peeled back to reveal a set of huge fangs. "Would you fight me?"

"I'd rather not, but if forced to, yes."

The expression on Azagoth's face became stony, sending a chill down her spine. "Will you beg?"

Beg? What a strange question. But it seemed to get a rise out of Hades, because he stiffened. "I...have never...begged."

"I know."

Hades dropped to the floor so fast and hard his kneecaps cracked on the stone tile. "Please, Azagoth," he began, his gaze downcast, his hand clasped against his thighs. "I've served you well, but if you want me to do better, I will. If you want to torture me every day for the rest of my life, I'll gladly submit. All I ask is that you allow me to see Cat between sessions." He lifted his head, and she had to stifle a cry at the liquid filling his eyes. "I am sorry about your son. His death must sit on your heart like a bruise, and if I could heal it, I would. I can only keep trying to make it up to you, but without Cat, I don't know how long I can survive to do that. Please, my lord, let me find the same happiness that you've found with Lilliana." His voice cracked with emotion. "*Please*."

Cat lost it. Truly, hopelessly, lost it. Sobbing, she sank down next to Hades and wrapped herself around him, needing to comfort him as much as she needed comfort. Her heart ached and her throat closed, and her skin tingled with the sense of goodness that radiated from Hades. Right now, he wasn't a fallen angel who ruled a demon purgatory. Right now he was a male, in pain and vulnerable, whose intentions were truly pure.

"Yeah, yeah," Azagoth muttered. "Fine. Get up. You have my blessing. That wasn't so hard, was it?"

Cat nearly burst with happiness as Hades blinked up at Azagoth. "Holy shit, so that's all I had to do was beg for your forgiveness?"

"Yep."

"So I could have done that centuries ago?"

"Yep." Azagoth's voice took on a haunted quality that struck Cat right in the heart. "All I ever wanted from you…after enough pain, of course…was an apology for taking my son's life."

Cat's eyes watered anew as Hades swallowed hard. "I am truly sorry, Azagoth."

And that fast, Azagoth's appearance returned to normal, the blood gone, his eyes glinting like gems. "I know."

Then, in a move that left Cat speechless, he offered a hand to Hades. Clasping Cat's hand first, Hades reached out with the other and allowed Azagoth to bring them to their feet. The two males locked gazes for just an instant, but in that brief, intense moment, something passed between them. Something she could only describe as mutual respect, and by the time Azagoth stepped back, she knew that this was the beginning of a brand new relationship between the two.

Hades tugged Cat close. "You know, I'm glad I didn't beg sooner, because if I had, I wouldn't have Cat."

"Yeah, well," Azagoth said wryly, "you *did* have Cat, and let me tell you, everyone in Sheoul-gra knows it."

A hot blush spread over Cat's face. Now she knew how Azagoth had learned about them. As the blush worked its way down her body, Hades planted a kiss on the top of her head, and the blush turned instantly to fierce, uncontrollable desire.

"I think," she said, "that everyone is going to know it again."

Azagoth cringed. "I'm out of here." He paused. "Before I go, do either of you know why my Seth statue is fucking itself?"

Cat nearly choked on her own saliva, and Hades held his hands up in denial. "No idea what you're talking about."

"Really." Azagoth's dubious expression said he wasn't buying it. "So you have absolutely no idea who glued Seth's penis to his ass?"

"Nope." Hades slid his hand to Cat's butt and gave her a playful pinch. "Didn't you say you were leaving?"

Muttering obscenities, Azagoth hotfooted it out of the apartment, and Cat turned to Hades with a sly smile. "You are very naughty."

Hades's eyes glittered as he trailed a finger along her cleavage. "You think?"

"I know." She went up on her toes and brushed her lips over his. "What do you say? Should we show everyone why they need to invest in earplugs?"

Hades tore open her robe and tugged her to him. "Earplugs? Baby, we're gonna need to soundproof this room after what I'm going to do to you."

"And what," she said, as she cupped his swelling erection, "would that be?"

"Everything."

"Promise?"

He reached around and slid his fingers between her cheeks as he lowered his mouth to hers. "Promise."

As it turned out, Hades kept his promise. And as it also turned out, everyone knew it.

* * * *

"Hello, Cataclysm."

Cat yelped in surprise as she whirled around to face the newcomer who had flashed into the courtyard in front of Azagoth's manor. She'd just been on her way to the Unfallen dorms to help Lilliana set up a new training program after spending an entire day in bed with Hades, and if she hurried, she could get back in time to join him in the shower.

"Reaver," she breathed. He stood there next to the fountain, his angelic glow radiating around him. "It's good to see you again. Azagoth is—"

"I'm not here for Azagoth." His deep voice rumbled through every cell in her body. "I'm here for you."

Her heart skipped a beat. Then another. And another, until it felt as if the organ was nothing but a shriveled husk in her chest. What if he was here to finally punish her for her stupidity in helping Gethel conspire against him?

"Me?" she croaked. "Why?"

"Because your actions in preventing the escape of millions of evil souls has earned you a reward." He smiled, his blue eyes sparkling. "I'm here to give you your wings back."

She sucked in a harsh breath as relief and joy filled her with such happiness that her body vibrated. He wasn't here to destroy her! But...why not?

"I don't mean to sound ungrateful, but...surely you understand what I did to you and your family. You know my history with Gethel, yes?"

Dark shadows flashed in his eyes, and she instantly regretted bringing up the evil bitch who had tried to start the apocalypse. "I am very well aware of your role in Gethel's machinations. But I also know you didn't realize the depths of her depravity until it was too late." The shadows disappeared. "She's paying for what she did, and you've paid the price as well."

"I'm not sure I have." She looked down at her bare feet as if her fresh blue nail polish would help her out. "I haven't apologized to you, either. I'm so sorry, Reaver. I didn't know what Gethel was planning, but I knew it wasn't good. I tried to go to Raphael, and he swore he'd look into it, but—"

"He didn't."

She shook her head miserably. "No."

"That's because he was tangled up in a million different plots to overthrow Heaven and screw me over," Reaver said. "I've always thought your sentence was too harsh, but once I learned that it was Raphael who sentenced you, it made sense. He wanted you out of Heaven because you knew too much."

"But I didn't know anything," she protested.

"I know. But he couldn't take any chances. Forcing your name on you was unnecessarily cruel, but not exactly a shock. He was, as one of my Seminus demon friends would say, a major dickmunch." He smirked. "Raphael's gotta be hating life right now."

No doubt. Thanks to Reaver and his brother Revenant, Raphael was sharing a ten by ten cage with Satan, Lucifer, and Gethel for the next thousand years. Wasn't long enough, in Cat's opinion.

A rabbit scampered across the courtyard. It might have been one that Reaver had brought to repopulate what had once been a dead realm. "So anyway," Reaver said after it disappeared under a bush, "you're forgiven. Come home, Cat. You'll even get your name back."

Once again, joy engulfed her, as if she'd been swallowed by the sun. The fact that Heaven wanted her back was all she'd wanted when she'd first arrived here, scared and lonely and full of regret. But now...now she was happy. Happier than she'd ever been in Heaven.

"Thank you, Reaver," she said. "But I'm afraid I'll have to turn down your offer."

One blond eyebrow shot up, but given that she'd just refused to get her wings and halo back, she thought he'd have been more surprised. "It's Hades, isn't it?"

Now she was the one who was surprised. "Ah...how did you know?"

"It makes sense." He cocked his head and looked at her with an intensity that made her feel positively naked. "Are you sure you want to stay here as an Unfallen? Your powers are muted, you're nearly as fragile as a human—"

"I'm sure. I don't need powers down here, and with people like Hades, Azagoth, Zhubaal, and Lilliana around me, I don't need to worry about my safety."

He nodded. "Cool. But know that if you change your mind, the offer will remain open as long as you don't do anything to betray Heaven or Earth. And you do understand that you could accept my offer and still be able to travel in the human and heavenly realms while living and working here in Sheoul-gra, yes?"

"I understand. But Hades resides in the Inner Sanctum, and as a fully haloed angel it would be far too dangerous for me to live there with him." She laid her hand on his forearm reassuringly but pulled it back before his Heavenly goodness burned her skin to ash. "Being Unfallen puts me at a serious disadvantage everywhere but here. Here, it's actually more protection than if I were an angel. I'm okay with it, Reaver. Really. Not everyone has to have badass superpowers to be something special."

"Can I at least give you the ability to choose your own name? Or give Nova back to you? It's a beautiful name."

A lump formed in her throat. That was the first time anyone had spoken her Heavenly name in months. It brought back memories, so many of them, both good and bad. But it was her past, not her future.

"Nah," she said. "I'm happy with who I am now. Raphael tried to shame me when he gave me my fallen angel name, but I won't let him do that anymore. I'll keep it to remind me to make wise choices."

"Then so be it." He pulled her into a brief embrace. "Be happy, Cataclysm."

Then he was gone, and she was holding empty air.

Chapter Twenty

One month after moving in with Hades, their new "crypt" was finally finished.

Azagoth had completely removed all restrictions on Hades, and they now had a decent house that matched the ancient Greek style of the rest of Sheoul-gra. Unfortunately, Hades had been so busy meting out punishment to the demons who had participated in the uprising that he hadn't had much time to enjoy it.

She'd taken today off from her new job working with the Unfallen, and she was going to make Hades do the same. They needed some quality time together, and she had the most amazing picnic planned.

He was at the Rot, as usual, which, besides their home, was the only place she was allowed to go in the Inner Sanctum. He'd taken her once to Cloud Cuckoo Land so she could thank the demons who had loaned her and Hades their home, but he'd made it clear that it was far too dangerous to do it again.

She finished dressing in a cute violet and black plaid skirt and a black tank top and gave the little wooden dog on Hades's desk a stroke along its back and tail, laughing when it snapped at her. It was a silly little ritual she'd developed every time she left the house. Hades had promised to make her a tiny cat to match, but he'd see if he could enchant it to purr instead of bite.

Rubbing her belly in a futile attempt to quell the anxious flutters, she stepped into the portal and arrived at the Rot a heartbeat later. She hated this place, couldn't help but think of the spider room every time she was there.

Malonius was at the entrance, and he gave her directions to some sort of classroom in the prison's upper tower where Hades was supposed to be dealing with a group of unruly incubi. She could only imagine what kind of punishments would be doled out to sex demons.

She climbed the narrow, winding stone staircase and found Hades sitting on a stage before a horrified audience. As she entered through the door behind the stage, Hades spoke, reading from a book in his hands.

"Fill me with your filthy pee stick." He paused for dramatic effect. "And lick my lush, melon-like boobies."

She tripped over her own feet. Pee stick? Boobies? What the hell?

"Come on, boy," Hades drawled, his voice pitched high as he read from what was clearly a woman's point-of-view. "My old pussy needs some young meat."

Cat cleared her voice to announce her presence, although, really, it was more like choking. Hades looked over his shoulder, his face split in a wide grin.

"Baby! Hey, it's good to see you." He waggled his brows as he gave her outfit a once-over. "It's especially good to see you in that."

She looked out at the roomful of demons, all human in appearance, as they sat in their too-small chairs, their eyes wild, their faces pale. Clearly, they were miserable.

"What *are* you doing?"

Hades held up the book. "I'm reading bad porn to a captive audience."

"Bad porn? *Bad?* That's a compliment. Whatever it is you're reading is horrifying. Whoever wrote it should be roasted slowly over a bed of coals."

Hades's grin widened. "I like the way you think." He waggled his brows. "Wanna play with my pee stick?"

She did, but not until he stopped calling it a pee stick. "Is that an actual offer or are you just having fun saying 'pee stick'?"

"Tell you what," he said, bounding to his feet. "What do you say we head back to my place, and I'll whip us up a nice pot of mac and cheese—the good kind in the blue box—and you can tell me what you like to call dicks."

"Does this mean we're done?" someone called out from the audience. "Please?"

Hades snorted. "Stay put. I'll get a sub in here." He glanced at his watch. "You only have twenty days and three hours left of listening to atrocious porn, and then you can go back to being the perverts you are." He waved, and they groaned. "See ya."

"That was kind of cruel," Cat said as they headed toward the portal that would take them to the house.

"But funny." He threw his arm around her and planted a kiss on the top of her head. "So? What's up? Are you breaking me out of prison for something good?"

"Yup." They entered the portal, but instead of passing her hand over the symbol that would take them to his place, she took them to Azagoth's realm. As they stepped out into the receiving room off the kitchen, she explained. "We're having a picnic."

He scowled. "Here?"

"Hardly." Taking his hand, she led him through the mansion and outside to the portal that could whisk them to the human realm. Azagoth had released his restrictions on Hades's travel, but so far, Hades hadn't taken advantage of his newfound freedom. It was past time he did.

He kept silent until they arrived at a sunlit meadow surrounded by mountains and looking out over a vast, azure lake. A bald eagle cast a shadow on the water as it flew overhead in search of a meal, and somewhere in the forest, a coyote yipped.

"Crater Lake." He inhaled the fragrant air, a bouquet of pine and summer wildflowers. "It looks just like the picture."

She'd done a lot of scouting to find the exact location where the photo had been taken, and Reaver had escorted her to keep her out of danger. Heck, Reaver had even arranged for her parents to meet her here a couple of days ago. They'd been sorry for the way they'd treated her, although her father had still been a little cool. But then, he'd always been a bit stuffy.

They'd been horrified by the thought of their daughter hooking up with the Jailor of Souls, had tried to make her reconsider going back to Heaven, and when she refused, they'd promised an open line of communication. Even her brothers and sisters had agreed to contact her. It was far more than she ever would have hoped for.

"Come on." Squeezing Hades's hand, she led him to the bottle of wine and basket of fried chicken, potato salad, and fruit she'd laid out on a red and white checkered blanket. Thanks to Reaver and a little invisibility spell, animals had left everything alone.

Hades sank down on the blanket, extending one leg and propping up the other to rest one arm casually across his knee. He looked absolutely edible like that, more at ease than she'd ever seen him.

"I've never been on a picnic before," he said as he peeked into the basket.

"I know. You told me once." Kneeling next to him, she poured two glasses of red wine and handed one to him. "My coworkers and I used to do it all the time in Heaven. Everything is so beautiful that it makes you want to be out in nature, enjoying every minute of it."

His gaze dropped, and even his blue hair managed to look sad. "Do you miss it?" he asked quietly, as if worried about her answer. "You gave up so much to be with me."

"No," she said fiercely, reaching over to tip his chin up so she could look him directly in the eyes. "I would have given up far more if I'd gone."

"I love you, Cat," he whispered. "I don't know what I did to deserve you, but I hope you know that I'd do it all over again to be with you. Thousands of years of loneliness was worth every second you've been in my life."

Something caught in her chest. Tears stung her eyes. That was the first time he'd told her he loved her.

"I love you, too," she rasped. "I can't believe I ever thought that Sheoul-gra couldn't be my home. You were right. Home is where the people who want you are."

"Mmm." He looked at her from over the rim of his glass, his gaze heating, focusing. Holding her in place.

Very slowly, he set down the glass and shifted so he was on his hands and knees, prowling toward her like a tiger with prey in its sights. Excitement shot through her. Electric, shivery excitement.

"Do you want me?" He pushed her backward, lowering his body over hers.

"Yes," she hissed as he scraped his fangs over her jugular. "Oh, yes."

One hand slid beneath her skirt and found her wet and ready. "Then take me home."

With so much love she thought she might burst, she very happily welcomed him home.

<<<<>>>>

Sign up for the 1001 Dark Nights Newsletter
and be entered to win a Tiffany Key necklace.

There's a contest every month!

Go to www.1001DarkNights.com to subscribe.

As a bonus, all newsletter subscribers will receive a free
1001 Dark Nights story

The First Night
by Lexi Blake & M.J. Rose

Turn the page for a full list of the
1001 Dark Nights fabulous novellas...

1001 Dark Nights

WICKED WOLF by Carrie Ann Ryan
A Redwood Pack Novella

WHEN IRISH EYES ARE HAUNTING by Heather Graham
A Krewe of Hunters Novella

EASY WITH YOU by Kristen Proby
A With Me In Seattle Novella

MASTER OF FREEDOM by Cherise Sinclair
A Mountain Masters Novella

CARESS OF PLEASURE by Julie Kenner
A Dark Pleasures Novella

ADORED by Lexi Blake
A Masters and Mercenaries Novella

HADES by Larissa Ione
A Demonica Novella

RAVAGED by Elisabeth Naughton
An Eternal Guardians Novella

DREAM OF YOU by Jennifer L. Armentrout
A Wait For You Novella

STRIPPED DOWN by Lorelei James
A Blacktop Cowboys ® Novella

RAGE/KILLIAN by Alexandra Ivy/Laura Wright
Bayou Heat Novellas

DRAGON KING by Donna Grant
A Dark Kings Novella

PURE WICKED by Shayla Black
A Wicked Lovers Novella

HARD AS STEEL by Laura Kaye
A Hard Ink/Raven Riders Crossover

STROKE OF MIDNIGHT by Lara Adrian
A Midnight Breed Novella

ALL HALLOWS EVE by Heather Graham
A Krewe of Hunters Novella

KISS THE FLAME by Christopher Rice
A Desire Exchange Novella

DARING HER LOVE by Melissa Foster
A Bradens Novella

TEASED by Rebecca Zanetti
A Dark Protectors Novella

THE PROMISE OF SURRENDER by Liliana Hart
A MacKenzie Family Novella

FOREVER WICKED by Shayla Black
A Wicked Lovers Novella

CRIMSON TWILIGHT by Heather Graham
A Krewe of Hunters Novella

CAPTURED IN SURRENDER by Liliana Hart
A MacKenzie Family Novella

SILENT BITE: A SCANGUARDS WEDDING by Tina Folsom
A Scanguards Vampire Novella

DUNGEON GAMES by Lexi Blake
A Masters and Mercenaries Novella

AZAGOTH by Larissa Ione
A Demonica Novella

NEED YOU NOW by Lisa Renee Jones
A Shattered Promises Series Prelude

SHOW ME, BABY by Cherise Sinclair
A Masters of the Shadowlands Novella

ROPED IN by Lorelei James
A Blacktop Cowboys ® Novella

TEMPTED BY MIDNIGHT by Lara Adrian
A Midnight Breed Novella

THE FLAME by Christopher Rice
A Desire Exchange Novella

CARESS OF DARKNESS by Julie Kenner
A Dark Pleasures Novella

Also from Evil Eye Concepts:

TAME ME by J. Kenner
A Stark International Novella

THE SURRENDER GATE By Christopher Rice
A Desire Exchange Novel

A BOUQUET FROM M. J. ROSE
A bundle including 6 novels and 1 short story collection

SERVICING THE TARGET By Cherise Sinclair
A Masters of the Shadowlands Novel

Bundles:
BUNDLE ONE
Includes Forever Wicked by Shayla Black
Crimson Twilight by Heather Graham
Captured in Surrender by Liliana Hart
Silent Bite by Tina Folsom

BUNDLE TWO
Includes Dungeon Games by Lexi Blake
Azagoth by Larissa Ione
Need You Now by Lisa Renee Jones
Show My, Baby by Cherise Sinclair

About Larissa Ione

Air Force veteran Larissa Ione traded in a career as a meteorologist to pursue her passion of writing. She has since published dozens of books, hit several bestseller lists, including the New York Times and USA Today, and has been nominated for a RITA award. She now spends her days in pajamas with her computer, strong coffee, and fictional worlds. She believes in celebrating everything, and would never be caught without a bottle of Champagne chilling in the fridge…just in case. After a dozen moves all over the country with her now-retired U.S. Coast Guard spouse, she is now settled in Wisconsin with her husband, her teenage son, a rescue cat named Vegas, and her very own hellhound, a King Shepherd named Hexe.

For more information about Larissa, visit www.larissaione.com.

Base Instincts

A Demonica Story (M/M)

By Larissa Ione

Coming Late 2015

According to the news, the weather system bearing down on Damon Slake was a proven killer.

But then, Slake was also a killer, and he could guaran-damn-tee that he was far more lethal than a thunderstorm.

Rain and hail pelted him as he stood outside one of several secret entrances to Thirst, a vampire nightclub that operated in the shadows of a human goth hangout called The Velvet Chain. Like most upscale vamp clubs, this one catered to all otherworldly beings, as well as humans who were willing to give themselves up as a snack for those who fed on blood. And, like most upscale vamp clubs, this place even had a medical clinic. Reputation was everything, and no club owner wanted to deal with a bunch of human deaths from overfeeding, or demon deaths from a drunken bar fight.

Which was smart, especially now, when the recent near-apocalypse had revealed the demon world to humans, causing tension, fear, and chaos. Humans were now in extermination mode, while demons were dealing with some sort of political shakeup in Sheoul, the realm humans called Hell. Slake had no idea what was going on in Sheoul, and frankly, he didn't care. He had a job to do, and he always completed his tasks.

After a lot of time and effort, he'd tracked his prey here, and it hadn't been easy. The wily succubus had covered her tracks well over the last couple of decades, but Slake had a knack for ferreting out secrets, and as good as the female named Fayle was at hiding, Slake was better at finding.

He entered the dimly-lit club, his status as a demon providing him with the ability to enter through a doorway only supernatural creatures could see. Instantly, the blare of rock music, the stench of sweating, dancing people, and the electric, sensual energy of sin assailed him. If he hadn't been on the job, he'd revel in the club scene, would be scoping out potential partners to take home for the night.

Partners like that sexy-as-hell medic propped against the wall near the medical station, his gaze sweeping the crowd with the intensity of a battle-wise soldier in enemy territory. Even from across the room, Slake could see the alertness in the guy's green eyes and the readiness for anything in the subtle tautness of his body.

And what a body it was. His black uniform stretched tight across his shoulders and abs, the rolled sleeves revealing thickly-muscled arms made to pin his partner to a mattress.

Slake had no idea if the dude was into males, females, or both, but the guy practically oozed confidence and sex. The medic crossed his arms across his broad chest, giving Slake a prime view of a sleeve of tattoos winding from his fingers to where they disappeared beneath his uniform at his biceps and reappeared at the top of his collar. The pattern ended just below his jaw, although Slake couldn't make out the individual designs. Damn, Slake loved tats.

He wondered what species of demon the guy was. He wasn't human; Slake's ability to distinguish a blue human aura from an orangey-red demon one made that clear. Not that Slake was picky when it came to bed mates, but he drew the line at fucking any species of demon that rated a five on the Ufelskala scale of evil. Fours were bad enough, but with a five, you never knew whether or not your partner was going to kill you after you came.

Or *before* you came, for that matter.

Reluctantly tearing his attention away from the medic, Slake strode through the club, his eyes peeled for his target. There were approximately a million and a half females milling about, but none resembled the petite, black-haired Asian in the picture he'd been given two months ago by his boss at Dire & Dyre, the law firm that employed him as an Acquirer. Yup, if someone wanted something or someone, Slake was the one sent to acquire it.

Except this job was different. This job was the one that would determine the course of the rest of his life.

And the rest of his *after*life.

But hey, as his boss pointed out, it was *only* his *soul* on the line.

The jackass.

He spied an empty booth near a little-used exit to the sewers and made a beeline to it, growling at a burly green-skinned demon who tried to slip into the seat ahead of Slake. The demon cursed, but one look at Slake's arsenal of weapons peeking out from beneath his leather jacket gave the guy second thoughts. Probably third thoughts, too.

A waiter brought Slake a double whiskey, neat, and he settled in, hoping his prey would show her pretty face. In the meantime, though, he didn't see any harm in checking out the medic at the rear of the club a little more.

That male was something special. Even his coloring was perfect. Not too tan, but not pale, and given the guy's reddish hair, shorter in the back than in the front, Slake would bet that close up, there would be some freckles waiting for the caress of a tongue.

Slake's mouth watered at the thought, and he had to shift to make a little more room in his leathers, but he didn't let his lust distract him from his mission. No, not when success meant freedom…and failure meant kissing his his soul goodbye.

He downed half his drink and reached for his cell phone just as the thing vibrated in his coat pocket. The name that flashed on the text screen was exactly who he'd been wanting to hear from for days. Hoping for good news from his favorite underworld spy, he tapped out a message.

Hey, Atrox, it's about time. Tell me you have an update on our prize.

He waited an unbearably long time for the reply. Atrox's fat fingers and long claws weren't exactly compatible with touchscreen keyboards. The reptilian demon had to use his knuckles to type, which Slake had found to be funny…until lizard boy used those knuckles to knock Slake on his ass.

Finally, the phone beeped with Atrox's incoming text. *Got a lead. One of the dudes I grilled last night is a regular at Thirst. Said he's seen the succubus several times in the company of a male with red hair and a sleeve of tats on his right arm.*

Well, now. Slake looked up at the hot medic and grinned.

This assignment had just gotten interesting.

On behalf of 1001 Dark Nights,
Liz Berry and M.J. Rose would like to thank ~

Steve Berry
Doug Scofield
Kim Guidroz
Jillian Stein
InkSlinger PR
Dan Slater
Asha Hossain
Chris Graham
Pamela Jamison
Jessica Johns
Dylan Stockton
Richard Blake
BookTrib After Dark
and Simon Lipskar

61215850R00094

Made in the USA
Lexington, KY
03 March 2017